Trilogy

The Box

By Freddy King

Table of Contents

<u>Chapter 1</u>

Following the sixties spy scandal and the Cuba crisis, Huntley Haverstock returned to his former life as Freddy Goodchild. During his involvement in the 'D' notice affair with Cuba and the foreign spies, all records of Freddy's existence had been destroyed by the foreign agents. The British Secret Services had restored his records following extensive investigations. Freddy and his friend Master Pilot Pinky James had given the secret services tremendous help in exposing infiltrators who had managed to establish themselves in many British Government departments. Only the government offices had any record of the help that they had given, and it could never be in the public domain. Freddy did, however, hold an M.B.E. for outstanding courage and contribution to Her Majesty's government. Many infiltrators in the Government services had been identified and arrested around the time of the Cuban crisis, and many new security measures had been introduced. It was hoped that the new measures would prevent any such infiltration in the future.

Freddy's help at that time had been invaluable and was the main reason for his recognition. He had remained with the secret services for some time following that affair and had been trained and promoted in the service. He had been involved in a number of investigations, but none as serious as his first. It seemed a long time after he joined the service, and he was due to leave. He was subject to recall as Huntley Haverstock when the service required him. It was a long time since he had seen his family, who had believed him dead, but unbeknown to Freddy, his family had died in that time. The family were led to believe that Freddy had died because when they enquired about him, they were told that there was no record of anyone of that name. He was now taking his leave and travelling home to Middlesbrough, wondering what lay ahead on taking up his earlier life. As he left London on his way to Middlesbrough he reflected that his circumstances were now totally different as he was now very wealthy and had the means to do what might have been unthinkable before. He travelled up the A1 in his Aston Martin DB4GT 'jet coupe', enjoying his 0-60 miles per hour acceleration in 6.4 seconds. It was very gratifying to think that his wealth had mainly come from the people who had tried to kill him. He hadn't heard from family or friends but had had contact with his former R.A.F. associates. As he drove through the driving rain he realised that he was quite nervous and apprehensive as he approached his home town.

3   Middlesbrough was an "Iron" town built on the local requirements of the Dorman and Long steel works. Previous to the steel works, the town was a halfway stage between Whitby Abbey and Durham Cathedral. Monks would rest there on their journeys between the Priories and access the ferry across the Tees River. "Would his house still be there, or had the family sold it off?" "What would the family think when he walked in on them?" these were just a few of the things that haunted him as he pulled up outside of his house in Linthorpe. The rain had eased to a fine drizzle as he walked up the path and stopped outside of his front door. For the first time, he had a look at the frontage, metal sheets covered the windows, and the door was sealed up by boards screwed into the door frame. A sign read, 'DANGER DO NOT ENTER'. Freddy was not going to be told that he could not enter his own house, no matter who had put up the sign. Freddy was in shock as he slowly went back to his car to get a tyre lever, and as he approached the front door, he wondered if his keys would still fit or had the locks had been changed as well.

He prised the board off across the lock and tried his key. It turned, and he pushed the door open. The door resisted from lack of use, but as it opened, the smell from inside stung his nostrils and sent him reeling backwards. He covered his face with a handkerchief as he levered off the remaining boards from the door frame, and he entered the house. Not one bit of furniture was left in the house; everything had been removed, and the house was littered with smashed pots, flower jars, ornaments and paperwork. The house had been totally emptied of furniture and carpets. It looked as if looters had cleared the place of everything of use. What was that smell? The downstairs rooms had the appearance of desolation, with dirt and mess spread all over the floors. What had happened here? After searching upstairs as well as down, he eventually looked in the cupboard under the stairs, and a hollow-eyed corpse met his gaze in an advanced state of decomposition. He was shocked, but there seemed to be something familiar about it. The stained clothing indicated that whoever this was had been shot or stabbed in the stomach and left to die a slow death trapped under the stairs. Freddy checked the clothing for any identification, but there was nothing. As he leaned across the corpse, he spotted a message written on the back of the door in blood: 'SECS has the answer'.

Freddy recalled that the only person who knew SECS was his cousin John. This had to be poor John, and the realisation made Freddy feels quite sick in his stomach. What was John doing here? John lived near Redcar, and they hadn't seen each other since childhood. It did not make sense that John should meet his end in Freddy's house in Middlesbrough. The message referred to the answers being in the secret safe. When they were young boys they had used the safe to keep their private things away from the girls and the adults that frequented the house. They kept their catapults and ammunition in there, their copies of 'naughty parchments' that parents must not see and their treasured copies of the Dandy and the Beano. Freddy went to the fireplace in the front room, and with the help of the tyre lever, he lifted the hearthstone. Underneath was the steel safe unscratched. Freddy and John were the only people to know that the safe code was grandmother's birthday. Freddy opened the safe, and inside, there was just one item: a stringed bag. Opening the bag, there was a letter stained with John's blood: 'As I write this, they are still in the house, so I hope to get it in SECS before they see me. They are looking for something but I don't know what. Your family thought that you were dead, and they are now, you are alone. They beat me up, but I told them nothing. Billy told me that you were still alive, and I came to sort the family affairs and I knew that you would come for GG's box. Good Luck. John' Poor John thought Freddy and he remembered fondly the good times that they had together and the scrapes that they got into.

He remembered with sad fondness. "So who were these people and what are they after?" thought Freddy, "could they be to do with the Cuban affair? Are they a new security threat? I will check with Sir George. Freddy put the letter into his pocket and looked into the bag. There was a scarf wrapped around something quite solid, but that was all there was. He unwrapped the scarf to find it inside a small metal box. Freddy shook it, and it contained something that rattled, but there seemed to be no lid, no lock, no seams, and so no way of getting into it. There was an inscription on the box that read: 'Albert Reuben 1865'. It meant nothing of significance to Freddy, but he remembered that his great-grandfather was called Albert Reuben, but 1865? That must have been what John was referring to, GG's box. Freddy thought back to John's final warning: maybe the house was being watched, and he may be being observed even now. He had better heed John's warning and get out quickly.

He left and headed for a safe house where he could contact Sir George. He made sure that he was not followed to the safe house, and he arrived safely to find the house empty. Following a call to Sir George, who was a departmental head of British Intelligence, Freddy was convinced that no security issues were involved. The only mystery was how to open the box to see what it contained and what was the significance of this strange box. After all it had cost his family and John their lives. He had to start by investigating 'Albert Reuben 1865'. 1865 must be important if it was Freddy's great grandfather, then he had to find out about him. He left the safe house and headed for Stockton-on-Tees, where his great-grandfather had lived before he moved to Park Lane in Middlesbrough. As he drove down the Stockton Road he contemplated cutting open the hollow box but worried about the damage he may do to the contents. He was deep in thought when a black Mercedes drew alongside, and as he glanced at it, he found himself looking down the barrel of a gun pointing right at him. The gunman was a front-seat passenger who indicated that he wanted Freddy to pull over to the roadside. In an instant his 'Jet Coupe' sprang into action, accelerating such that it left the Mercedes standing. Freddy tried to read the number plate in his rearview mirror as he sped away, but he only managed to get a part of it. He thought that it could be traced quite quickly as there were not too many cars of that sort in the northeast of the country. The Mercedes faded into the distance and at the first opportunity, he left the road unseen around a bend. His training came to him automatically, and he applied his knowledge to lose his followers.

Sure that he was no longer being tracked, he stopped and contacted Government security services on his car radio. They came back to him with three possible owners, one a doctor, another a car dealer, and the third an M.P. It was dark when he arrived in Stockton, having taken a wide detour to lose his followers. He stopped outside of Lol Davison's house. Lol and Freddy were childhood friends and Freddy hoped that Lol still lived here and could put him up for the night. Lol opened the door, and his mouth dropped open, "You are supposed to be dead. Great to see you come in. What have you been up to? Where have you been all this time?" "I'll just park the car round the back, out of sight." Lol met Freddy as he parked the car and showed him in through the back door. "I know that it is a bit presumptuous, but could you put me up for the night?" "Of course," said Lol, "I have a spare room. Come on, I'll show you." They came back down to the lounge, and Lol opened up a vintage bottle of wine. "You have arrived at a good time. I have just taken delivery of a few cases of Italian wines, and you can help me test them out." Lol was full of questions because he had been told that Freddy had died while serving in the R.A.F. Freddy told him as much of the events as he could but much of his story was still classified information. As the evening progressed, they relaxed and sampled the wines. They talked about the good old days when they were kids in the early hours of the morning. Lol was fascinated to find out what Freddy would do now and was very keen to help if he could. Freddy suggested that they sleep on it and take it up the next morning. They retired for the night. The following morning at breakfast, Freddy told Lol that he would take a room at the Swallow Hotel in Stockton. He thanked Lol for his help and assured him that he would keep him in touch and that if he needed help, he would get back to him after he learned more about the box and why it was so important. The box, after all, had cost people their lives. He said that he would contact Lol as soon as he knew the room number at the Swallow and after he had booked in. With that, Freddy left and headed for Stockton High Street.

Chapter 2

True to his word, Freddy called Lol and told him his room number. Freddy did not fully unpack but he picked up the box to study it but could find no way of getting the thing open. There were no seams and no obvious construction signs but there was something inside which rattled when shaken. Freddy wrapped the box in a small face cloth and put it into his toiletry bag and took the bag to the front desk. He called for the Hotel manager and arranged for the bag to be placed inside the hotel safe with strict instructions that no other member of staff was to be informed of its existence and no one other than Freddy could collect it or be told about it being there. "What if you need it to be collected?" enquired the manager. "Unless I collect it in person, no one must know anything about it. Is that clear? You must follow these instructions to the letter!" The manager assured Freddy that he would let no one other than himself open the safe, and no one would be told that Freddy had deposited anything in the safe.

Back in his room Freddy sat and thought about recent events and why people should be following him. It had to be the box that made him a target, and that meant that the box had to have some great value. The people following would stop at nothing to get their hands on the box. That was clear, but who were they? Freddy's thoughts were interrupted by the room telephone, and it was Lol. "I am in a phone box just off the High Street, and I need to see you urgently." Lol sounded very shaken, "What is the problem?" "My front door was smashed down, and a gang burst into the house. I was out the back and escaped out of the garden door and climbed out over the garden fence. I can't go back, and they are still in there and from where I was, I could see that they were turning the house upside down. They were wrecking the place!" "Did they see you or know where you are?" asked Freddy. "No, I was out before they could see me." "Which phone box are you in? Never mind, go round to the restaurant on Church Road, and I will come and get you. Try and keep out of sight and watch for my car coming for you."

Freddy put the phone down and went to his car and headed for Church Road. He drove slowly down the road, and he saw Lol run out of an alleyway. Freddy opened the passenger down, and without fully stopping, he saw Lol jump in. They headed quite slowly without interfering with other road users and headed for the main road out of Stockton. After ten miles, it was clear that no pursuers had followed them. Slowly, Freddy drove back to the Swallow Hotel, and they went to Freddy's room without being seen by anyone. "This is nastier than I ever could have imagined. What the hell is going on, Freddy?" "I have very little idea at the moment, but I think that it all has to do with the little box and whatever is inside of it." The phone rang, and it was Sir George Curswell, the head of secret services in London. Freddy answered and confirmed coded identities, "We have had some people making enquiries about Freddy Goodchild, and we have been unable to establish who initiated the enquiries, but they were made through a contracted enquiry agent who could not confirm who they were being paid by. We, of course, denied any knowledge of a Freddy Goodchild, and there was no reference to Huntley at all. We need to meet. I am in Leeds tomorrow. Can you be at the Leeds headquarters about two in the afternoon?" "Of course, Sir George, I will be there," as he replied, the phone went dead. "Was that Sir George that did that, or was the call intercepted?" thought Freddy.

He quickly packed his things and went to see the manager to let him know that he still required the room for an indefinite period, but he would not be returning to occupy it tonight. He picked up his bag and called for Lol, and they set off for Leeds. Freddy was applying all his training to be sure that they were not able to be followed. After much detouring and evasive manoeuvres, they arrived at the Wetherby Hotel and booked adjacent rooms. In the restaurant, Freddy and Lol considered their situation, "I'm sorry to have involved you in this, whatever it is, Lol."

"From what I now know of the situation, you could not have possibly foreseen such an aggressive and persistent group following you. The box doesn't look like any metal that I am aware of, and it isn't gold, platinum, silver or even steel. I would never have thought that such a small metal box would be so valuable to someone that they would go to such desperate lengths." replied Lol. "Well, I have caused you to be temporarily homeless, but I will be able after my meeting tomorrow to arrange a solution for you. In the meantime, let's try to have a pleasant evening while we have the chance. Do you still have contact with the crowd that we used to knock about with?" They talked well into the early hours about the old times and characters that they used to know. They enjoyed the hotel hospitality and the food and drink, but eventually, they retired for the night.

Freddy had an early start and left without waking Lol, but he left a note to say the he would be back in the late afternoon. He headed for Leeds H.Q. as he had a lot of work to do before Sir George arrived. Records could provide some information that could throw some light on the metal box and it's origins and possibly the people who were trying to get their hands on it. In the records section, he trawled through file after file with little success when Bert, one of the Leeds staff, came into the room with some information on metallurgical research, which he thought might be of help. Freddy thanked Bert and opened the file to find the cover sheet describing the file content on metallurgy development programs, but the rest of the file was empty. All project information had been removed but there was a name at the top of the file cover, hardly distinguishable, which startled Freddy. The name was that of his great-grandfather, Albert Reuben Goodchild. He knew little of his family history, but he knew the name well, and that was all that he knew about his great-grandfather. The rest

15

of the file was blank, apart from a few reference numbers that someone had attempted to obliterate.

The file room door opened to reveal Sir George framed in the doorway, "There you are, Huntley!" Sir George always used Freddy's code name. "What are you up to?" Freddy greeted him and suggested that they grab a coffee and find a private office. They settled down with their fresh coffees in a secured interview room with the door locked, "Have you found anything of significance, Sir George?" "No, but I think that you have a lot to tell me from your intensity. I had very little to go on." "Neither did I, but Bert came up with this file, which you may find to be of interest." Freddy opened the file and passed it over to Sir George. He noticed the security level of the file, and he was obviously astounded that a file of that level could have been compromised in such a way. "I will take this and make some enquiries. This is a very serious matter that must involve people with a high-security clearance. Tell me more about your story." Freddy spent a long time explaining all that had happened and how Lol had become involved. They talked for over an hour, exploring all the possible scenarios or reasons for the past events, but everything led back every time to the mysterious box. "I'll take the box to the boffins and see what they can make of it and come up with. As Lol appears to have been drawn into this, I will leave it up to you how much you involve him. In light of what has happened of late, you are now back on the pay role and you can allocate what is needed to accommodate Lol. This is now an official enquiry, Huntley Haverstock, so you are both bound to the regulations, so make Lol fully aware of all requirements." With that, they set off to pick up Lol from the Wetherby Hotel and the box from the Swallow.

On arrival at the Swallow Hotel, the manager was in quite a state. Lol was trying to calm him down. I didn't tell them anything, Mr. Goodchild, but they wouldn't listen, and they took your room key and tore the place apart. It is a total mess." "Did the safe contents come into the conversation?" "No, I said that you had kept yourself to yourself since you arrived and that I knew nothing about you. Who were they, Mr. Goodchild? They were real nasty pieces of work." "I'm afraid that we do not know, but we will make good any damages, and I will take my package without delay. Many thanks for your discretion. You did very well." Huntley settled the hotel bill, and all three set off for London with the box safely in their possession. They left the cars at

Leeds H.Q., and they were escorted in a security car to the Leeds rail station to complete their journey.

They were met at Kings Cross station by a security team to ensure that no one knew of their arrival or journey through London. It was a pleasant day as they travelled and they were sufficiently relaxed after their rail journey to take in the views as they headed for Sir George's office. On arrival, Sir George offered them the office suite accommodation, which they both gracefully accepted. Freddy had stayed there before when he and Pinky James had helped security previously. Freddy explained to Lol that the suites were five-star accommodations and fully stocked with refreshments. Lol was very pleased with his room, and he had never seen such luxury. Sir George left them and set off with the box to the scientific development department.

After Sir George left, Freddy and Lol discussed the immediate future. "Look, I didn't expect to involve you in this mess, Lol, but now that you are we need to decide if you want to get out now or become even more involved." "It is a no-brainer, and I'm not letting these thugs get away with trashing my home and causing so much distress. It is now that mates need to stand up and be counted,

and I am standing up. What do you want me to do?"
I don't know yet, but it is great to have you on
board. I will get Sir George to make you legit with
salary and a place you can call for now. You can if
you want to stay in one of the billets in London if
you prefer. The billets are very good, and I have one
near here on the Embankment, I can get you in there
if you would like that." Lol nodded. "Okay, that's
settled. We'll take a stroll around there now. I will
let security know what we are doing so Sir George
can get in touch." They walked along Whitehall and
called in to pick up a car from the security garages.
They continued by car to the Embankment billets.
When they arrived, Freddy got the keys from the
attendant and showed Lol his new quarters.

Lol was very impressed, and after a full tour of
the place, they set off by car to Bond Street to do
some serious shopping.

It was a new experience for Lol to charge
everything to an account that someone else would
settle for him, so he bought one or two things for
the sheer hell of it. London was new to Lol, so
Freddy gave him an extensive tour of the city 'up
west' and points of interest. They enjoyed a coffee
in the '2 i's' coffee bar in Soho, where Freddy
introduced him to the resident singers Vince Eager,

Wee Willy Harris and Ricky Towns. They walked through Piccadilly to Leicester Square, on to St. James Park and back to Whitehall. They enjoyed the walk as the sun was warm for an autumn day, and there was no wind. When they got back, they had to cool down for a while before going to Sir George's office. As they entered, they were greeted by Sir George, "Well! What do those boffins get paid for? I've no idea. Not one of them could get anywhere with that confounded box of yours. They tried to cut it, burn it, hammered it and even tried to open it with acids. Not even a scratch on it and it just rattled at them. None of them has any idea about it's contents. What have you two been up to?" "I have booked Lol into an Embankment billet near mine, done some shopping and taken in some of the local points of interest. I take it that the box provided no answers?" "Nothing," was the reply, "So, Lol have decided to see this through for the time being, so we will have to put him on the team if that is okay with you." "They were also my thoughts," said Freddy, "he will be working with me, so I will arrange all necessary training and instruction. Is that okay with you, Sir?" "Yes, that's fine but I can't help you in where to start. These people have left us without any clues as any leads have been a dead end for contractors who haven't a clue. It is up to you to get going. I will allocate a team for you to use as back-up or researchers. We have ensured that your John has a decent burial. My office and resources are ready to support you when needed as this smacks of our enquiries on one of the joint previous cases. National security might be again at risk. Go to it, lads and keep me informed." "Thank you, Sir. We will keep in full communication." With that, they left and walked back to the Embankment. Still, the weather had changed for the worse, and they were relieved to sit down to a terrific Italian meal at the restaurant adjacent to their billets overlooking Westminster Bridge.

Chapter 3

It was nice for Freddy to meet the restaurant staff again and renew old friendships. As they ate Freddy mulled over the possible starting points of enquiry and decided that he should start with finding all he could about Albert Reuben Goodchild. They finished their meal, and at the records office, Freddy trawled through the files and found that Albert had worked in the Dorman and Long research and development department at the Lackenby Steelworks in Middlesbrough. He had specialised in Bessemer Steel sampling, but that is where all traces stopped. No references, no further information and missing file content. The last entry referred to 1897. Someone had been through this information and, for some reason, taken all further relevant documentation. In another section, Freddy found that in the same year as the last entry, Albert had disappeared. There were no reports of accidents, deaths or travel details. It was as if he had left the planet Earth, never to be seen again. No wonder the family history was so sparse and full of supposition and myth. So it all led to the Middlesbrough Steel works, and that was where they had to start.

The very next day, they visited Jackie Beal, who worked in the I.C.I. metallurgy department. He told them of an old cooperation that had been established years ago on a project that had been abandoned. He told them that the only place that might have some information would be at Lackenby Works. Now, they had a starting point, but they had to be prepared for anything in the future, so they went to a local weapons section and collected a full weapons pack, just in case. They had travelled by train to Leeds and had collected Freddy's car to drive on to Middlesbrough and there they had booked into the Highfield Hotel. It was late as they drove back through lashing rain to the hotel, and the northeast wind forced them to have the car heating on full blast.

Freddy commented that the north was always a few degrees colder than London and the south but even he was shocked at the change in conditions. They certainly would not like to walk anywhere in this sort of weather. After a good night's sleep and a hearty breakfast they set off on the dull Sunday morning to visit Don Fielding, a friend of Lol's who also worked at one time at I.C.I. along with Jackie. He lived on the Beechwood Estate. Freddy was alert to anyone who may be following them, but he was sure that they were alone. The estate was very quiet, as always, on a Sunday morning. Freddy parked the car on a field behind Don's house and they walked through the cut into the housing.

Lol knocked at the door, but it was some time before there was any answer. Lol thought that Don might not be at home, but after a few more knocks, the door opened to reveal someone who had had a very good night out and was showing the after-effects. "Good grief! I thought it was ghosts, and I haven't seen you two for years. What's up? Come in and find a place to sit if you can. They both knew their way around the house, and they went into the lounge. A body came to life on the settee, rubbed its eyes and staggered out of the front door. "Who was that?" asked Lol. "No idea!" said Don, who was busy in the kitchen trying to find everything needed to make a cup of tea. The place was a mess. "Good party?" "I think so," said Don, "I will let you know later when I wake up a bit."

Don came into the lounge. He had managed to make the tea and even found some biscuits. "Help yourselves, and I couldn't be responsible for pouring tea this morning." As he spoke, Don threw some debris on the floor to make room for a sit-down, and he flopped into an armchair. The teas were poured, and Freddy made some small talk before asking Don about metallurgy and, in particular, the qualities that applied to research in the nineteenth century at I.C.I. "Funny you should ask about that. Is it important?" "It has cost people their lives and may be of national security."

"When I was working in the R & D section at I.C.I. Wilton, I came across an old enquiry from a team at Dorman and Long. I took particular notice because I saw the name Goodchild on the file cover. A relation of yours?" Freddy nodded. "It appears that Dorman and Long's labs were asking I.C.I. to confirm some incomplete steel particulars. The file reply was strange in that they said no tests were conclusive but then they refused them any further help. That is just not like any I.C.I. response to possible development material. They would be falling all over themselves to develop and pinch it if it showed promise, but just to dismiss an enquiry of that nature was not an I.C.I. option that I would think of. I looked into it but couldn't find anything in our archives about it. All things like that were recorded and kept, but there was nothing. Wait, Old Stan Barker would have worked there about that time, and his grandson has just retired from the same department as him. Now he lives on Sutton

Estate just over the field there. I have his address somewhere." "That's great, Don. We need to speak to him as soon as possible." Don left the room and soon returned with an address. They thanked him and apologised for disturbing his Sunday morning snooze time, and they left. They assured Don that they would be in touch again and let him know what had happened. Don was quite excited as they left to see Stan's grandson. His recovery was remarkable.

As they approached the address they had been given, the door opened, and Alan Barker was about to leave. He came to a halt as he turned and saw the two boys approaching. Alan was not in a cooperative mood but Freddy explained why they were calling on him, and Freddy was not going to be put off by the frosty welcome. He took out his official security card and displayed it for Alan to see. The change was dramatic, from being aggressive and uncooperative to a fearful character who had something to hide. He re-entered the house, followed by Freddy and Lol. No words were spoken, but it wasn't necessary as Alan's nerve snapped, and he started to bluster and deny everything and anything. Freddy stared at him, and eventually, Alan went on to admit that he had passed on some industrial information but was under great pressure. "Stop there!" said Freddy, "what information and to who?" "It was only that one time, three guys demanded that I pass them a Dorman and Long enquiry sheet that was in a file that I was working on. They said that something really nasty would happen to me if I did not do as they said. They were big lads, all of them, so I didn't argue. That's all!" "Who were these guys?" "Some contractor who I had seen on site who worked from his shed in Grangetown. He is called Gordon Trattles. I had no choice. What else could I do? It wasn't important stuff anyway, and it was only a Dorman and Long steel enquiry."

"Just important enough to get people killed. Where's your phone? Alan pointed to the hall. Freddy called the local police, identifying himself with the operation code and had Alan taken away for further interrogation. Lol had done some building work with Trattles and was fully aware that he had dealings with the criminal fraternity. "We may need backup at this point Lol so we may have to delay going after this guy until it arrives.

They made their way back to the Highfield Hotel and had some lunch. The sun shone on the hotel gardens as Freddy considered how long it would take for Sir George to get back to him. He had left a message for him, but he thought that the office weekend programme would mean that he would not hear from him until after lunch on Monday. Meetings with the ministers on Monday morning always took priority and always lasted until they took lunch, no matter how trivial the subject matter was. As Freddy and Lol were leaving the next morning, a member of the hotel staff gave Freddy a message from the local police. It read, 'the contractor had been collecting the information on behalf of a professor Pescolari who is based in Geneva at the Fontain & Brach laboratories. "A lead at last, and it takes us to Geneva. We have no further need to bother the local contractor. I'll let H.Q. know and we can take a little weekend relaxation. How about going to Redcar and striking up old acquaintances at some of the old haunts?" Lol, agreed, and they set off for the coast. Redcar had not changed much since Freddy had last spent some time there. Everything was in full swing on a Sunday morning. The ghost train and other amusements were doing great business. Screams emanated from the interior of the ghost train and not all were children's screams. As they queued up to get an ice cream, Lol spotted a familiar face in the crowd, "Don't look now but outside of the rock shop is one of the men who trashed my house!"

"We'll get our ice creams and walk up the seafront to the street near the R.N.L.I. lifeboat station. We can hide in the cut-through to the high street and see if he follows us." Having got their ice creams, they casually strolled up the seafront and turned into the alleyway leading to the high street. As soon as they turned the corner, they ran twenty or so yards to an alleyway junction. Freddy went left and Lol right. Seconds passed before they heard the approaching sound of hurried steps. As the follower got level with the junction, Lol shouted, and the man turned to face him. Freddy tackled him from behind and took the man to the floor with a resounding crash. For the first time, Freddy used his handcuffs to restrain someone. He had bound the man with hands behind his back. "I'll hold him until you get back Lol, dial 999 and get the police here as quick as you can. Tell them it is a code MS." Lol ran to the high street but found that the call box was damaged, so he went to the Red Lion hotel, where the manager was very helpful. And before Lol could get back to Freddy, he could already hear the approaching police sirens showing that their response to his call had been extremely rapid. The man was taken into custody, and the Chief Constable was informed that the secret services would be in touch to take the prisoner as soon as possible. Another message went to Sir George informing him of the situation.

The Chief Constable was not too happy, but after his questions were answered, he complied without any further objections. The prisoner carried no identification and refused to make any comment or answer any questions. Freddy insisted that the man was to be charged with aggravated burglary and that he should be held until he was taken by security. Freddy addressed the Chief Constable, "Thank you for your co-operation, and I am sure that he is safe in your custody. We haven't time to waste on his sort, and he will be taken where he will answer the charges." They left Redcar, headed back to the Highfield Hotel where they checked out and headed back to London. They were sure that they weren't followed, but just to be certain, they detoured and took standard evasive procedures.

<u>Chapter 4</u>

Back at the Embankment, they were just in time to join Mario in a great meal in the cafe before retiring for the night after a very busy day. Freddy left information for Sir George before falling into a welcome, deep but disturbed sleep. The next morning, they were having breakfast in Antonio's cafe when they were approached by a messenger from Sir George with news of the prisoner left in custody with the Redcar police. He was dead! He had been found dead that very morning, hanging in his cell. No further information had been given. The messenger left them both shocked and confused as they considered how a prisoner could be allowed to have the means to kill himself whilst in custody, that is, assuming it was suicide. "Who and what are we dealing with for a man to take his life over such a menial charge? It doesn't make sense when any lawyer worth the title would have had him out of jail in minutes and probably with only a caution. There has to be something about this that we haven't discovered, so important for such drastic behaviour. It can only mean that there is a lot of money at stake somehow. Sir George told me that the boffins could not make any impression on the box, not even a scratch. That leads me to think that the contents are not as important as the box itself. The properties and composition of the box must be the target of this group following us. Our professor, Pescolari, must have some ideas about it. I'll go to H.Q., but if you want to stay and have a wander…." Lol, cut him off in mid-sentence, "No! I'm with you, I need to know what this is about as much as you do." "Okay, let's go to the records department and see if they can come up with something on this Pescolari chap."

When they arrived at records Henry already had made some important findings on the professor. It was confirmed that Pescolari was a leading metallurgical chemist working for the F.A.K. Foundation based in Geneva. "So it looks as if we are on the right track at last. We need to go over to Geneva and meet this guy face to face and see what he knows about the box. We will go to the office and update Sir George." Lol nodded in agreement. Sir George could not allocate any agents from his post in the U.K.. Still, he agreed to alert any agents in the area of Geneva to the investigation and ask for any relevant knowledge to be relayed back to the U.K. They had no way of setting a plan, but they knew that backup was available if required. They both agreed that the best approach would be to meet the professor at his home for the best results, but everything depended on his response.

They were packed very quickly and on the way to the airport for the flight to Geneva, a driver had been sent to pick them up. Pescolari worked in Geneva, and after they arrived in the afternoon, they picked up their hire car and headed for the Quai Gustave Ador, where the professor worked. They had some photographs of him, but they were quite old copies, and they hoped that they could still recognise him. They passed the Quai Gustave and headed for the house in Avenue De L'Aurore. Freddy drove passed the house to see if there were any signs of life, but all was quiet, so he parked a little way away in the Avenue Du Printemps. They parked and waited for the professor to arrive home. Freddy hoped that the information on the professor was correct and that his English was good as Freddy could speak some French but it was far from fluent. After waiting for a while, Freddy felt that things were being left to chance by just waiting. They had to have the element of surprise and that could not be achieved from the car.

"Come on, we are going in. We will leave the car here and walk to his house before he gets home. That gives him less chance of spotting us and doing a runner." Lol nodded, and they headed for the house. It was a three story building with metal fences and a large metal gate which opened smoothly.

They checked for people watching as they entered the gates, but it was a very quiet area, and there was no one in sight. The front day was locked, so they walked slowly around the house until they spotted a slightly open window. It was a small window but large enough when opened for Lol to lean inside and open the large window beside it. Once inside, they closed the window and started to look around the house. The main bedrooms were downstairs, along with a bathroom and toilet. Upstairs was a large sitting room with excellent views of the front of the building. No one could approach the house without being seen from the sitting room. It overlooked the large gate and it gave a panoramic view of the road outside. They settled down to wait, but they did not need to wait long before a car stopped and parked outside of the gate. The driver got out and came through the big gate and approached the door. From the photographs, they recognised that the driver was indeed Professor Pescotari. They heard the key in the front door lock and the door opening and closing, then footsteps on the stairs.

Freddy stood behind the sitting room door, and Lol stood flat against the wall on the other side. The professor opened the door and walked over to the side table. He heard the door close behind him and turned to find himself facing two strangers. "Please do not be alarmed, professor. We do not mean you any harm or discomfort. We just need to talk to you." The professor sank slowly onto the settee, clearly in shock. "We are sorry to startle you in this way, but we are only here to ask you about the men that you hired in the U.K. We are investigating certain matters on behalf of Her Majesties Services, and we need your help." It took some time for the professor to recover his composure and comprehend the situation.

Freddy and Lol seated themselves opposite the professor and waited for a response. "How did you get into my house?" he asked. "You left a window open. I must explain, as I said previously, that we are acting on behalf of the U.K. Government with respect to murder and serious assault associated with another very serious matter." "I have nothing to do with such things. The people I hired said that they were private investigators. I needed someone in the U.K. to be able to access information on a company called I.C.I. I made it clear that they should respect the Laws of the U.K., but if they could find me any information on a rumour that metal had been discovered that could be changed or altered without the use of heat or chemicals, then they would be well rewarded. The notion of such a metal is ludicrous, but I had to follow up on it as the financial and commercial benefits would be outstanding. They assured me that they knew of this and could find proof of such a metal, so I paid them a handsome sum of money to pay any expenses. My employer was only too pleased to back me with the necessary finances. You mentioned murder, and surely these people were not involved?" Freddy thought for a while, going back over the conversation with Alan and the pressure that he had been under at the time. Freddy concluded that there was no evidence of any wrongdoing.

The Redcar suicide man had no apparent connection to them. The professor interrupted his thoughts, "I will take you to talk to my employer, Monsieur Le Blanc, if you wish and he will confirm all that I have told you. After a short pause, Freddy said, "I do not think that it will be necessary to do that. We are sorry to have met you in such a manner, but before we leave you, we will need the paper that they sent to you." The professor immediately got up and opened his briefcase. Taking a paper from it he handed it to Freddy. The professor said, "We found nothing of value in the report to support or explain the attributes, so you are very welcome to take it but it did give some validation to the claim that such a metal does exist." "Thank you, professor. We will leave you in peace and hope that we did not cause you too much distress." The professor assured them that he understood as he accompanied them to their car. They parted in congenial terms. When they reached the airport Freddy contacted Sir George to keep him up to date with their progress.

They caught the evening flight to London. Lol was surprised that Freddy had taken Pescotti at his word, but Freddy explained that the information on the I.C.I. report was as much as they now needed, and though there might be some doubt about Pescotti, it could wait. When they arrived at Sir Georges' office, he was busy reading the I.C.I. report, and Freddy joined him. The name at the top was Albert, but there was also a reference number which was hand written. Most of the report was typed. No information was helpful as to the nature of the metallurgical enquiry, and there were no details of any formula. In faint pencil at the bottom, barely legible was "ref to me". "I wonder what that is", pondered Sir George. "Who is me, I wonder," said Freddy. "I will get records on to that straight away". Sir George picked up the phone and gave instructions there and then. "We will wait for a response." "Tea, coffee?"

They sat drinking their coffee and related past events, expressing possibilities. Still, it was becoming very clear that there were two factions involved, one obviously more desperate and violent than the other. They had no clues as to who the second group were. It wasn't long before the phone rang, and Sir George answered. "It appears M.C. is the project manager in charge at that time". He died some years ago but his grandson was working at I.C.I. quite recently. He is called Jason Condor after his grandfather, Martin Jason Condor. It looks as if we have a possible line of enquiry." The report from records showed that there was lots of information relating to Jason Condor. He had been named as a member of a number of suspect groups which had led to a number of criminal convictions. The latest five showed two convictions for fraud, one for serious theft and two involving grievous bodily harm. He was not known for operating alone, and he was constantly involved in some sort of gang activity. There was no record of a fixed address, and he had not been known to be active for some time. In fact, there was no record of him being in the United Kingdom at this time. Strangely, there was no record of him having left the country. He had become a ghost figure. "It looks as if we've hit the jackpot, Huntley," said Sir George. "It is a definite lead, Lol and I will start a trace on him. Can you find if any recent cases in England fit his Modus Operandus? We'll go to the last place he was sighted and take it from there." Back in records, Freddy found that the last address for Condor was Park Road South in Middlesbrough. Freddy and Lol made their way back to the Tees Valley and started making enquiries door to door and came across someone who had known him well. "Yes, I know Jason, we were good mates and regulars at the Park Hotel." "What is your name?" "Sorry, I'm Bill Noakes." "We are trying to find out what happened to Jason and where he is now. Do you know where we can find him?" "I'm glad that someone is taking this seriously. I reported Jason missing ages ago. You said that you are from security services?" Freddy nodded. "Jason was really excited. He told me that he had hit the jackpot and would soon have more money than we had ever seen. The last time that I saw him, he was on his way to South Bank to meet some 'High Rollers' as he called them. We never saw or heard from him again." "Have you any idea who he was meeting?" "All that he said was that they were foreign guys, and they were all millionaires, and he had something that they would pay a lot of money for."

"Any idea what?" enquired Lol. "Something that he had found out about at work. He was a Lab assistant at I.C.I. I can't tell you any more about it because he kept it close to his chest. He was always after the big breaks and he wasn't particular how he got it. One thing that might help, and I've always kept it, it was the last thing connecting me with Jason, is the book of matches with the meeting time on it. Here, you can have it if it helps you find him." "Thank you for your help. We will let you know if we find him." Freddy and Lol left Bill after he gave them the book of matches. The logo on the matches was Wilton Social Club, so that was where they headed.

Many years ago, Freddy had been a guest at the club, he had been invited to play golf and squash by a former member. He had been impressed by the many facilities that the club provided for its members, but on the social side, there had been indications of rifts between members and talk of underhand and devious dealings. Freddy had not changed his opinion since those times, and he always regarded the place with deep suspicion. The membership had been very closed to outsiders and visitors had been treated with resentment and a dismissive attitude, distinctly unfriendly. Their investigations were not going to be straightforward, and they would need help from a present-day member. Lol was a great help in this matter as he was still in contact with his tradesmen friends who had contacts with the I.C.I. club, one who actually lived in Redcar.

Chapter 5

Redcar is a seaside resort on the northeast coast. The arcades and pleasure rides were plentiful when Freddy and Lol were children. They remembered the Rock shop that made and sold Redcar Rock and the ice cream parlours where the luxurious "Knickerboca Glories" could be savoured and enjoyed. With these memories in mind, they headed for the Red Lion Hotel to book a couple of rooms for the night. It had been many years since they both went riding at the Lobster horse riding stables, so after they got their room keys, they headed for the Lobster Inn.

It was a public house that had regular local support but was popular for visiting clients. At the rear of the pub, there were extensive stables and horses owned by the Lobster but many kept their horses stabled there. It was early evening, but they hadn't eaten all day, so on arrival, they ordered the Lobster Inn special, fish and chips. The fish was caught fresh every day and bought from the fishing Cobles on the Redcar beach. They were delicious, and not one word was spoken until they had both cleared their plates. They washed the meal down with a pint of bitterness and spent a pleasant evening remembering the good times they had and sadly commented on the fact that the stables had been gone such a long time. They would not be galloping down the beach again on Lobster horses. As they soaked up the atmosphere, Lol attracted Freddy's attention to someone entering the bar. It was Don Fisher, the one that they had come to try and find. "That's a stroke of luck, Freddy. Don has found us, and nothing could be more natural than our meeting him." Lol got up and approached the bar at the same time as Don. "It's Don, isn't it? Fancy meeting you after all this time. I'm here with my friend Freddy over at the table there." Lol, pointed towards Freddy. "I don't know if you two have met before, but let's get our drinks and join him at the table. Don approached the table, "Pleased to meet you, Freddy", shaking Freddy's hand, "I never expected to see Lol here tonight. What a chance, eh? I don't think I have seen Lol since we converted the Alexander Hotel into flats." "Yes", said Lol. "Freddy helped me out on that job with the electric wiring." "Great, so you are in the trade as well, Freddy?" "No, just a 'go for' for Lol." "What are you two doing in Redcar then?" "We were just slumming and reminiscing about the old riding school, so we thought that we would come and see what it is like now," said Lol. "Sorry to say that the stables were demolished years ago." said Don, "It just wasn't paying its way anymore, and the boss here had no choice but to close it and extend the bar space." They continued chatting about the jobs that they had done together for some time. Lol steered the conversation, eventually, to the I.C.I. Social club. "Last time I was there, I partnered with Jason Condor in a golf four. Do you ever get there now, Don?" "I will be there tomorrow in a squash match. Do you want to come and give me some support?" "That would be fun. Are we both invited?" "Of course, shall we say six o'clock tomorrow evening? Look, it's been great seeing you again and chatting about old times, but that's my date that has just come in, so I will see you both tomorrow. Cheers, lads."

Freddy looked at Lol and said, "How well do you know Fisher?" "Oh, he is okay. We have done lots of work together, and he has always been reliable. Why do you ask?" "I'm not sure, and there was just something that wasn't right about that guy and the way he greeted us. You are probably right, and maybe I am just being over-sensitive. We are dealing with some very dangerous people, and you never know how far their influence can reach." They finished their drinks and set off to walk back to the Red Lion Hotel. As they approached the front entrance, there was a sudden movement in the shadows of the alleyway. Freddy reacted quickly and ran into the shadows where he had seen the movement, but there was no one to be seen and no signs of anything out of place. Lol ran after him, "What was it?" "I don't know. There is nothing to see now, but I'm sure that someone was there watching us arrive." "You are just spooked. I didn't see anything." "Yes, you are probably right. Let's get inside away from this cold sea breeze, which doesn't help."

The following day was spent sightseeing and losing money in the 'one-armed bandits' in the arcades. After a tea of the local fish and chips, they set off for the I.C.I. Club to meet Don and he was waiting for them as they drove up to the club car park. "I'm glad that you are early there's just enough time to have a snifter in the members bar." Don led the way into a very comfortable bar area, went around behind the bar, and poured three drinks. After sitting down with their whiskies, Don went on about his forthcoming match as the boys drank their drinks.

<u>Chapter 6</u>

Freddy woke up to find himself lying on a very lumpy and uncomfortable camp bed. He had no idea where he was or how he had got there. He looked around to see Lol lying on a trestle table. He could hear voices and realised that people were in another adjoining room. He looked around for a door, and there was just the one in the room where the boys had been put. Freddy heard someone say, "They should be out for the count for another good half hour with the dose that Don gave them." Other voices were quite muffled and muted. Freddy got to Lol and shook him. It took a few minutes for him to come round. They discussed their situation, and Freddy informed Lol about the comment from the next room. They were in a sports store room, and there were no windows. The only light was from a dirty skylight in the ceiling. They knew that they had to get out and get away as fast as they could, and they could distinguish about five different voices in the other room, which made it unlikely that they could be overpowering that number of captors.

They seemed to wait an age before they heard a voice say, "That sounds like the boss has arrived.

You two wait here while Jed and I go to meet him." "Is that wise, there's two of them in there and only two of us here?" "They will still be dead to the world for some time yet." A door slammed shut, and they heard someone say, "Grindley will be pleased with us when he sees that we have those two in there." "Quick Lol, get on your table and moan as if you are not much longer for this world." Lol got on the trestle table and started moaning like a cow in agonising labour. Freddy was even concerned that Lol was actually in pain. There was a cupboard behind the door which would give height advantage. Grabbing a hockey stick, he climbed up behind the door.

"Louder," said Freddy. There was a commotion and some argument next door, but Freddy heard the lock turn in the door, and it opened to reveal two men. Lol's moaning and thrashing commanded both of their attention. As they moved towards Lol, Freddy timed his attack to perfection. His feet landed on the back of the first one sending him smashing into the squash racket shelves while catching the other one with a mighty blow on the back of his neck. He went down and stayed down. Freddy quickly recovered his balance and quickly got to the other man, but he was also unconscious.

"Come on, Lol, let's get out of here." They locked the stock room door behind them, leaving the two sleeping men inside and went out through the oposite door in the outer room.

They found themselves in the squash court corridor and the emergency exit was straight ahead of them. Once outside, they made their way around to the rear of the social centre and then onto the car park. A group of men were near Freddy's car, and it had to be the gang and the tall man giving instructions had to be Gimly or Grindley, the boss. They heard the boss say, "Take me to them. There will be no distractions this time, and we will have that box. You two get the car keys and hide their car, and we don't want any nosy parkers asking silly questions." The group headed for the social club entrance, and the boys watched as they disappeared through the club door. The boys came up behind the two men left in the car park, and they took them completely by surprise. The men were left stunned as they grabbed the car keys and dashed to the car, which started immediately and they headed off as fast as they could. "That was a lucky escape, Freddy, and you certainly sorted those two out in the stock room. It could have been very bad for us if we hadn't escaped when we did." "I couldn't afford

to mess it up, and we need to get to a safe house
straight away.

I will get someone to pick up our gear from the
Red Lion and I need to inform Sir George of the
situation. We now have a definite lead, and there
was something very familiar about that Grimly or
Grindly guy." As they headed for the safe house,
Lol went very quiet, and Freddy realised that shock
had set in with Lol. After all, he was not trained or
even used to such happenings. Freddy was
conscious that Lol had fully realised how serious
this was, and it was certainly no game. These guys
play for keeps. Freddy pulled into a farm entrance
just outside of Ilkley and drove straight into a barn.
He got out and closed the barn doors so that no
prying eyes could see the car. They went into the
farmhouse. The far was deserted and looked very
run down from the outside, but inside, it had every
facility one could think of. Freddy located the
service radio set and opened the emergency
channel, which sprang into life immediately. After a
short delay, Freddy heard Sir George respond and
quickly confirmed the identification. Freddy gave a
full report of recent events including his suspicions
about the boss called Grimly or whatever his name
was. Sir George told Freddy to stay at the farm and

that he would send help as soon as he could. Freddy signed off, and as he did, he remembered the vehicle parked in the middle of the car park at the social club. He couldn't be certain, but he would wait for Sir George before he took any further action. They concentrated on settling down for the time being and set about making themselves comfortable. Freddy asked Lol if he was going to stay with him on this mission, knowing that events had badly shaken Lol. "I think that things are getting a bit too intense for me, and I haven't seen my Uncle Joe in France for a long time." "I fully understand Lol and I think that it is a wise move to get out of the country for a while. You have been a great help to me, and I appreciate all that you have done, but enough is enough. When this is all over, we will meet up again and have a great vacation on the company funds. I will arrange all the necessary travel for your visit to France, and you won't need to worry about anything. The company owes you. It would be wise not to go back to Stockton and your place until we find and deal with these people and bring them to justice. Best to stay here until arrangements are complete, and then you can set off without being concerned that anyone has spotted you."

"How soon can you arrange it, Freddy?" "Give me an hour." Freddy went to the radio and contacted H.Q. And came back within half an hour to find Lol fast asleep. The best thing for him, thought Freddy. He left him to sleep to get over some of the shock. Freddy left the paperwork and full itinerary for Lol's forthcoming journey to France. It was arranged that he would leave this evening and be in France tonight with a secure escort. The escort arrived within the hour and Lol was taken to Leeds Bradford airport in secret to board without delay on a charter flight to France. Lol found that a complete set of luggage had been provided. Freddy waved a fond farewell to Lol as the aircraft took to the skies, and then he headed back to the farm. As he approached, he could see lights at the farmhouse. Freddy got close enough to see people searching from room to room. Freddy circled the building and saw two vehicles parked out of sight a short distance from the farm. Obviously, they did not want to be seen from the road as anyone approached the safe house. It had to be Grimly's men or whatever his name was. The farm was surely not safe any more. What to do? Challenge them? Not a good idea! Sneak up and try to identify some of them. How did they know where he was? Freddy sat in his car with his brain churning away at all the possibilities when he saw seven or eight men leaving the farmhouse and making their way back to their waiting vehicles. It was already quite dark and Freddy decided to turn the tables on them and follow to see where they were based or to whom they were reporting.

He reversed his car into a farm track entrance and waited. Soon, he saw the headlights getting closer, and he hoped that he had hidden the car sufficiently to go unnoticed. The cars passed, and he could see as they did that no one even glanced his way. He followed them without turning on his car lights so as not to be seen following. They were not too far ahead, and their lights on full beam lit the road very well, for Freddy not to need his lights. They eventually left the minor roads and headed onto the M1. Dropping back a little before he got to the M1, Freddy turned on his lights. Much to his surprise, the group headed south and did not vary from that heading at all. As time progressed, it became clear that they were heading for London. Freddy's mind buzzed with questions and possibilities as to who these people were and where they were heading. He followed them through London, and he was shocked, to say the least when he realised that they were directly headed for the

Government buildings. As they entered White Hall, Freddy passed the entrance and stopped a short distance away. He noticed that the group was not even challenged as they went through the check-in gate.

Freddy headed for Sir George at his office. Sir George was not there, so Freddy occupied one of the suites at the office and spent the night there. He did not sleep much as the gravity of this development left him wondering if his previous experiences with infiltrators were to be repeated. It was now very obvious that the leaks were within the organisation, and that is how they knew where he was at all times after past reports to H.Q. He had a fitful night and hardly slept, but he washed and shaved before Sir George arrived shortly before eight-o-clock. It was Sir George's turn to be shocked to see Freddy sitting in his desk chair as he entered. "Before you say anything, Sir George, I want to know how the so-called gang knew that I was at the safe house?" "What? Wher's Lol?" "I sent him away yesterday." "What do you mean, they knew where you were? Did you get followed?" "No one followed me. They were given the information from H.Q., And they arrived in force. How else could they have known and so quickly?"

"You are not suggesting that I gave them the information? Freddy did not answer. "I certainly did not pass any information to any third party." "We have been in this situation before, Sir George. Only you and I knew where we were. No, not just you. I contacted H.Q. to make arrangements for Lol to travel.

We have a 'mole' in the department." "After our last purge, I know that we have no one here who would leek information outside of the service." "Exactly!" Freddy went on to tell him why he was back in London and that the assailants were here in central London. Sir George sat down with a thump. "Are you telling me...." "Yes, I am. We have a very violent and determined organisation within this building trying to get their hands on that box, which I want back in my hands without delay." "I have it safe here," said Sir George.

"Nothing is safe here. I want it back now." Sir George did not argue. He went straight to his safe and handed the box to Freddy. "I have a lot of checking to do, Sir George. If you want to come for an Italian meal at about seven this evening at my embankment house, I will be able to tell you more."

With that, Freddy left the office to make his enquiries. At seven o'clock precisely Sir George knocked on the door, "Come in, Sir, Italian food as promised from downstairs, enjoy." A few pleasantries were exchanged during the meal, but not a lot was said. As they finished their meal and washed it down with some Montepulciano Da Bruzzo Freddy started to tell of his findings. "I managed to identify those men who followed me and who I followed back here. They are all genuine Servicemen who were following orders from Captain Simmerby, and I misheard when I thought it was Grimley. He is part of the research department team and is head of research into metals. It all starts to make some sort of sense until one considers that they are willing to kill to get their hands on the box, including service personnel. They knew full well that I was a member of your team, but I was a target." "Well, I have some news for you. After you left my office this morning my safe was broken into while I was out. You were right when you said that nothing was safe here. Who dares to give orders to break into my office and breach security protocol? If it is this Simmerby chap, I'll have his guts for garters." Sir George picked up the phone in Freddy's room and demanded to see Simmerby. Simmerby was his junior service member by a number of grades, and

Sir George was in the mood to tear Simmerby to pieces, probably to end his career in the service.

Back at the office, Simmerby was waiting for Sir George who gathered himself before inviting him in. "Sit down, Simmerby. I have a few questions for you." "Of course, sir, how can I help you? It is great to meet you at last" Freddy mused that it could be his last. Sir George continued, "You have been up north recently. Might I ask what you were doing there?" "I was following your instructions, Sir." "What instructions?" "Is it wise to discuss it here, Sir?" He glanced at Freddy. "I asked you what instructions, Simmerby, and when I ask a question, I want a reply." He was visibly having trouble keeping his temper with this man. Simmerby sensed the danger, "You ordered my team and I to obtain some box by any means required. You said it was of national security and that anyone who obstructed was to be illuminated." "Did you kill Freddy's cousin John?" "We had to deal harshly with him as he would not cooperate." "And the house in Stockton?" "We thought that it might be hidden there, Sir." "Did you also pursue Huntley Haverstock here and threaten his life?" "Those were your orders, Sir." "I gave you no such instructions, Simmerby, and you had better start telling me how you dare to act in such a way." "But sir, I have your written orders, including breaking into your safe to get the box." Sir George was silent, obviously struggling with his anger and frustration. "You say that you have written instructions and orders from Sir George. Can you confirm this?" asked Freddy. Simmerby showed his resentment at being questioned by Freddy, but he sulkily nodded. Sir George called for security, waiting outside of his office door, "You will escort Simmerby to his office and return with him here as soon as you can. Do not let him out of your sight. Simmerby, you need to produce your evidence. You will go with security and return here with your written orders, now!"

Security marched Simmerby out of the office, and they returned within half an hour. Security was aware that Simmerby was under arrest and they had made sure that he was not out of their sight for one second. Simmerby handed Sir George a file marked 'Top Secret'. "You will disregard any previous orders and remain with security until I call for you. Security, take him out and keep your eyes on him until I require you to bring him back." As the door closed behind them, he opened the 'Top Secret' file. As he read page after page with increased intensity, the shock on Sir George's face became more apparent.

"What is it, Sir?" He was slow to respond, but eventually, he stared at Freddy and he was visibly shaken, "These orders are all apparently signed by me. The signatures on the first view are mine, but that cannot be as I didn't write any of this stuff, and I certainly did not order Huntley Haverstock to be illuminated." Freddy stared back. The shock on their faces showed a dawning realisation that, yet again, their department had been infiltrated by a third party. "This needs a full investigation. I'll get Simmerby back in again, and I want you to fill in any points that I might leave out." Back in the office, Simmerby was becoming decidedly more uncomfortable, "Sir, I don't understand. Your orders were very specific and I carried them out with my team to the best that I could." "How did you come by these orders?" "From you, sir." "Damn it, man, I issued no such orders and come to think of it, I haven't had to contact your office for some time. I'll ask you again: how did you receive these orders?" "In the dispatch box from your office, sir." "Who brought them to you?" "Well, that was the unusual thing, sir. They came by a courier, but as it was top secret, we did not think it too strange." "Be more specific, man, was he a Government courier or contract?" "The only identification was on his black uniform in the form of a Raven. More than that, I don't know, sir, but I ran a check on the signatures on the orders, and they all checked out." "Very well, Simerby, that will be all for the moment, but I want you and your team to stand down completely until I contact you again. Do you understand?"

"Yes, sir." "Simmerby, I want all of your available agents to investigate who this courier was and who he was working for, and I want to be informed at all stages. You have jeopardised and embarrassed this office. You have murdered and threatened innocent people and harrassed my team, and until I get to the bottom of this, your team have your direct orders to find that courier, and you are suspended from all other activities until we catch this man. You and your office will keep me fully informed daily, and I will not tolerate any delay in any information reaching me. Is that clear?" Simmer by left with the security guards.

"Well, Huntley, I think that we have been here before. They have used our people to do their dirty work for them, and at least your friend, Lol, will be able to come and go as he pleases now. I trust that you will let him know that the heat is off him?" "Of course I will, sir. He will be most relieved." "You are back on full operations from now, so stay in London and make this your headquarters for the duration. Do you still have the box?" "I have access to it at any time, sir. It is safe and will remain, so I can assure you, sir." "Everything seems to revolve around that thing. It has all of our boffins totally foxed, but if we knew its' properties, then it might help us to understand what is so important about it. Will you let me have it? We need to find out something that will help." "It is getting late, sir, and I will bring it first thing in the morning." "Thank you, Huntley." Freddy left the office and headed for his apartment on the Embankment. He was looking forward to a bit of peaceful rest for a change.

Chapter 7

The following day, Huntley had the box ready to take into the office. He had not seen any news in the media or on television for some time so he turned on his television while he had his breakfast. He placed the box beside the TV so that he would be certain not to forget it. He went to make his morning coffee and returned to watch the latest news, but as he watched the TV, the box caught his eye. It was changing shape and size. Tentatively, Huntley touched the box, but there was nothing to indicate that anything was happening, no vibration, no heat and no sound. He picked up the box, and the box stopped any change or process that he had watched. To his amazement, it was no longer a box, and it would certainly no longer fit into his pocket. It was the shape and size of a rugby ball. He shook it, and he heard the same rattle that he had heard before. Huntley found a shopping bag and popped the ball into it. He needed to get this thing to Sir George as soon as possible, so he left for the office.

Sir George was amazed by the changes to the box and questioned Huntley about the circumstances, but it confounded them both. One advantage now was that with a little disguise, the box was unrecognisable to any prospective usurper. The news came that Simmerby's office had received a new message, and the courier had been detained. "Well, bring the courier here." said Sir George, "We need to question him. I cannot believe these people. You even have to wipe their noses for them. Whatever happened to the initiative?" The courier arrived under guard and was ushered into a vacant interview room. Sir George left him there to increase pressure on him before he and Huntley entered the room to interview him. Sir George led the questioning but had instructed Huntley to intervene if required. "What is your name?" "Billings," came the reply. "For whom do you work?" "Raven couriers." "Who sent this message?" Sir George had not even opened the envelope to see what it contained. "It came by wire from abroad." "Where from, man?" "It came via Paris, from Geneva and a Mr Zeute." "Do you know who this man is?" "No, we just deliver the messages that we are given."

Huntley looked at Sir George and indicated that he needed to speak to him in private, and they both left the room. Huntley reminded him of the Geneva connection that he and Lol have looked into. "I don't believe that this billings chap has any information to give us, but the company might

know more. Shall I check them out with a visit?"
"Yes, and I will see if I can get a trace of the origin
of this message. I will just follow up on our Billings
man, just in case." Huntley got the Raven couriers'
address and headed over to their office. Sir George
had read the message and informed Huntley that it
contained his signature on immediate inspection.
The instructions contained were even more insistent
on Simmerby getting hold of the box to await
further instructions. Huntley arrived at Raven's
couriers and met up with the owner, Jed Bates. Jed
was very cooperative and gave all the details he had
on the sender of the messages. He had no details of
the Geneva office other than the stamp "Geneva,"
but he knew the Paris office well and arranged a
call. Jed spoke to Paris and obtained a P.O. Box in
Geneva." "I am sorry that we can't be more specific,
but there is no way that we can source the P.O.
Box." "You have been a great help, thank you. I
appreciate all of your efforts."

Huntley left and returned to the office and
confirmed that Billings knew nothing of interest in
this case, and they released him to return to Raven
Couriers. In the meantime, Sir George had
instructed Simmerby to reply to the message to
confirm that he had the box in his possession but to

delay for four days. This would give Huntley time to visit Geneva, obtain any information, and, hopefully, be there when there was a pick up at the P.O. Box. The journey was uneventful, but while he was there, Huntley just had to do some shopping at Stanley's of Geneva. He also had to visit Krane's Seneca shop. Fashions were changing quickly in the sixties, and while Huntley was not a particular follower of fashion, he liked to keep up with the trends when he could. For his shopping he went to Auburn Pants Factory Store and bought a few things for himself. The time came to get down to business, so he headed for the Favette Postal Centre on Ovid Street. He needed to familiarise himself with the area before the courier or whoever was planning on picking up the message from London.

He identified the actual P.O. Box, checked the surrounding streets, and then waited. It was late afternoon of the fifth day that a young boy picked up the message from the counter clerk. Huntley shadowed the boy while in the line at the counter and heard the boy say that it needed to be posted to London. He wasn't able to hear the box number, and he immediately discounted any involvement by the boy. Obviously, he was just a messenger. The post office was reluctant to divulge any information on the box number, but after much negotiation and explanation of his mission, they gave him what he wanted. He set off for London without delay. He was shocked as he travelled and considered the number, which, in fact, sounded very much like a diplomatic box number. It was confirmed later that it was a diplomatic box, but it had been de-commissioned years ago by whom no one knew, and there was no record in the file.

It was sited in the old building quadrangle, which meant if an observation point was to be set up it would have to be inside the building. Huntley arranged discrete access to the old building and chose an office directly opposite the old P.O. Box. As he sat in the window, he turned to look at the empty office, it looked as if everyone had just got up and left it as it was. Pens were still on the desk, an empty tea cup next to a loaded typewriter and a file on safety open on a desk. He chuckled at the thought of the Marie Celest office. Dust covered everything, and his gaze settled on his footprints on the floor when he spotted a movement in the quadrangle. A post office worker approached and dropped the re-directed message into the P.O. Box. Huntley had a skeleton key and could have checked the contents of the box but chose not to as it might risk his cover. He decided to wait and see who would come to collect it and open the box. Time hung heavily as he waited and waited. The day passed into evening and then twilight, and as darkness approached, Huntley decided that the time to pounce on anyone collecting had passed, but he waited again until dawn was imminent. 'Enough,' he thought and risking it, he headed for the box to check the message.

He quickly left the office before it got light and went into the quadrangle and he opened the box with the special key to find that the box was empty. 'How could he have missed anyone opening the box? It wasn't possible?' he thought. 'I haven't missed anyone, but how is the box empty?' He looked now at any possibility of accessing the box. He checked the wall, but there was no sign of any break or lack of solidity. He checked the bottom of the box for any crevices that might conceal the message. Locking the box again, he realised how tired he was, so he headed for his flat to get some necessary sleep. Almost immediately after falling asleep, it seemed, the telephone rang. It was daylight, and Sir George was calling him, "Come to the office immediately!" The phone went dead.

Huntley got out of bed, washed and dressed, and was in the office within the hour.

On arrival, Simmerby was sitting opposite Sir George, "At last Huntley, come in and sit down. Simmerby here has another message with my name on it with instructions to deliver the box to the Ministry Mailing office. Did you see who it was who collected the message from Geneva?" Huntley just shook his head thinking it better not to give any report until Simmerby was out of the way. There was a delay, but Sir George got the feeling that Huntley was not happy giving any information in front of outsiders, so Simmerby was dismissed with instructions to return to the office at 3 o'clock in the afternoon. As soon as it was clear, Huntley reported on his experiences. "No one came to pick up the message. No one! The box was empty, but no one collected it! And how did Simmerby get hold of it? I sat in that dusty office nearly all night and saw no one after the postie delivered it. Wait, what am I thinking of? That office was filthy from years of neglect, but the bottom of the P.O. Box was as clean as a whistle. No dust leaves or rubbish of any sort. It has been accessed and used regularly, and the only way that could happen without being seen is from the inside of the building, but how?" Sir

George picked up the phone, "I will get the plans of the old building sent up straight away. Meanwhile, I need to find out who is getting hold of my stationery and who signs my signature. This is a very dangerous matter which has the potential to breach all office communications with disastrous consequences. I'll get the plans to you as soon as I can. You go and take a break after your night vigil. You look shattered."

Huntley made his excuses, left the office, and headed for the downstairs restaurant for his breakfast below his flat on the Embankment. Mario's coffee would surely wake him up a bit. He realised that he hadn't had a proper meal for days. He ordered and enjoyed his Fusilli Gratinati washed down with a large glass of Chianti followed by a large cup of Italian coffee. He was glad to have a break from the investigation, even for a few hours and leave Sir George to get on with things himself. This was a very complicated investigation, and nothing made any sense. What was happening, how were things happening, who was behind it all, and why was the box so important? He thought that the best plan was to find out how that P.O. Box was accessed so secretly. If he found the access point, it might give a clue as to who was involved. He slowly relaxed as he sipped his coffee but his attention was quickly diverted as he heard his name being mentioned to Mario.

He looked up to see a very attractive brunette making her way to his table. "Do you mind if I join you, Huntley? I have a file for you from records." She sat down before Huntley could say a word. "You have me at an advantage as I do not know your name." "I'm sorry, I should have introduced myself. My name is Judy Blain from the Office of records. I was told to give this file in person." "How did you find me here?" "Sir George told me that I would most likely find you eating in this cafe." Judy passed the file across the table, and Huntley looked hard at her. He was somewhat concerned by this approach and the fact that she was still sitting at the table as if she was waiting for something. He considered his options, but as he did so, she pondered an expresso. "Shouldn't you be getting back?" "I am on my lunch break now, so I thought that I would combine the two things and have something to eat here. What would you recommend?" She ordered Maccheroni Al Quatro Formaggi on Huntley's advice, and they both ate with very little conversation. Judy did not eat all of the generous portions of the meal, and she quite suddenly got up and said, "We will have to do this sometime again. It was very nice meeting you." She fidgeted with her handbag and left.

Chapter 8

Huntley did not know what to make of this surprising encounter. Was Sir George playing Cupid? No, never, it wasn't in his character, but why would he send her and not page him as agreed? He felt that Judy had not been totally honest with him, but he could see no reason, in retrospect, to be concerned. Huntley opened the file to find the plans of the old building adjacent to the quadrangle. The P.O. Boxes backed onto the old post room from where the post was sorted and delivered to the various departments and offices. That would explain how someone could access the boxes unseen and with frequent and recent use would also explain the dust-free bottom of the box. Someone was accessing from inside of the old building, and Huntley had to get into the place to see what the setup was and possibly gain some clues as to who it was going in and out of there without someone else knowing. He would get the keys and go this afternoon. He looked again at the plan and noticed that the old building was adjacent to offices still in use. A corridor separated these offices, but it was clear from the plan that the corridor had been blocked and that the passage was not in use or accessible, at least at first glance. It had been blocked off years ago.

It never ceased to amaze Huntley that such resources could be mothballed without any obvious reason or even discussion with other staff. This disused area must be worth a fortune in real estate and it was standing empty. He shrugged and thought it was no use to reason why. He just had to get in there and find out for himself. Later Huntley was back at his vantage point in the old quadrangle but this time armed with keys to access the whole building. He unlocked the door next to the P.O. Box and went into a corridor. As he walked he looked back to the entrance to see that the only evidence of any traffic in there was his footprints. As he went from corridor to corridor, they were all the same, with dust undisturbed for seasons no sign of anyone being here at all. Eventually, he found the postroom. The door swung open, and Huntley hesitated to look at the floor. Behind the boxes and on the other side of the room, the floor was covered by footprints, but none from the door on this side of the room. The prints led to a door on the other side of the room, but the plans did not show any door other than the one that he had used. The corridor separating the old building from the new was behind that wall, and no access was shown from that corridor. Huntley tried the door, but the handle did not give, and there was no sign of a lock on this side. It was obviously secured on the other side of the corridor. He quickly left the post room, making sure that it was locked and headed for the new building to look for access from that side. He could not remember who occupied that department of the ministry, and as he approached, he could see the plaque read 'Ministry of Overseas Development'.

Huntley thought that he could not risk searching the building whilst it was occupied, so he planned to come back with the security officers later that evening. Out of curiosity, he telephoned records to talk to Judy Blain but they said that there was no one of that name in that department. Huntley called Sir George to inform him of events and the mysterious Judy Blain, but on hearing that name, he told Huntley that he knew of her in the Ministry of Overseas Development. "It looks as if you are on the right track. I am going to be with you this evening when you search, and I have a vested interest in this caper." Huntley was taken by surprise, Sir George very rarely got involved in the fieldwork after the Cuban affair.

Sir George was obviously very rattled by this case. Sir George arranged the search for eight pm. The autumn had the chill of winter as they entered the Overseas ministry accompanied by two armed security guards. The concierge at the desk confirmed that the building was empty and that Judy Balin had a ground-floor office. He led the way to her office but told them that there was no corridor on that side of the building. Blain's office had a definite feminine touch, with fresh flowers on her desk beside her nameplate and the bureau. The curtains were patterned with a delicate flower design. The office lacked windows but was well-lit when they switched on the lights. The desk was tidy, the 'In Tray' was empty, and the 'Out Tray' contained just one file. Against the wall where the corridor should have been was a beautiful antique bookcase filled with an astonishing variety of topics. Huntley picked up the file in the out tray and opened it to find him looking at himself. It was a large photograph taken in an Italian restaurant with a nice bottle of Chianti in the foreground. He had been totally unaware of being photographed, and obviously, it had been taken recently. Then he remembered Judy fiddling with her handbag earlier in the day, obviously really. 'So that was the purpose of their meeting today.' he thought. It hadn't been Sir George who sent her so it had to be the person who was pretending to be him but who was it? Yet again, whoever it was knew of the plans made in Sir George's office, but how? Freddy continued reading the file and the full report of the meeting in the restaurant. He searched the file for any clue as to who the report was made for but there were no names or references to any individual. Huntley replaced the file into the tray and took out the building plan to show Sir George where the corridor should be, and the concierge confirmed that the wall behind the bookcase was where the corridor should be. They inspected the wall but could not find any door or breaks where there could be access.

Huntley walked to the bookcase and tripped over the luxurious mat that was in front of it. He did not want to leave any trace of their visit, so he bent down to straighten the mat, but as he did, he noticed, where it was dislodged, tread marks underneath. He pulled the mat away from the bookcase to reveal tracks caused by the movement of the bookcase itself. He was about to ask for help in moving it but as he put pressure on it, it moved very easily to expose a hidden door behind. The door was not locked and opened smoothly into the corridor. As they entered the darkness of the corridor, the security guards lit their bright torches to reveal a trail of footprints that led to a barred door. Huntley raised the bar to open the door to the old postroom. It came as no surprise, and now they knew how and who had collected the messages, but who were they intended for? They carefully made sure that no trace of their visit was visible, and they left the building, binding the concierge to complete silence and secrecy. Sir George warned of the serious consequences if the concierge broke his promise.

Back in the office, Sir George set a twenty-four-hour watch on Judy Blain's activities and monitoring of telephone calls and communications to her office. They now had to wait for results, but in the meantime, a full history report on Judy Balin was set in motion. The one thing that puzzled Huntley was why Judy had lied about being in the records department. She must have known that her lie would be found out, so he decided to call on her first thing in the morning under the pretext of seeing her again.

The next day, bright and early, Huntley luxuriated over an Italian breakfast before going to see Judy but was interrupted when Mario called him to the telephone. It was Sir George, "Miss Balin is on the move and in some sort of panic. You will not be able to intercept her as she has already shaken off our team at the airport. From air traffic control, she appears to be heading for Ireland. We have alerted our agents over there, and her flight is being monitored. I will see you when you get into the office." The phone went dead and Huntley went back to his breakfast that had been kept warm by Mario. "More trouble with the ladies' boss?" asked Mario. "You don't know how right you are, Mario." Huntley headed for the office after finishing his meal but decided to check the box that seemed to be at the heart of this matter. There seemed to be a definite atmosphere when he got to the laboratory.

People were reluctant to communicate with Huntley, so he headed straight to the senior official. "What has gone on here?" demanded Huntley. "Are Huntley!" said Professor Murton, "We did not expect to see you." "Obviously not, but I want to see the work report on my box, and I would like to see it now." "Well, that might not be possible," said Murton. "Why not?" "We are still working on it." "Well, I want to see your work, and I want to see the box, and I will not take no for an answer." "But" "No buts, lead on now!" "I don't know if I am authorised to let you." "Stop now. Lead on." The professor was reluctant, but he knew that Huntley had the backing of Sir George, so he led him to the central courtyard.

The sight before him left Huntley speechless. The huge, shiny object before him was still the shape of a rugby ball but hundreds of times bigger. It was the size of a London double-decker bus. They both stood for what seemed ages before Huntley asked what had happened, but the professor had no explanation. "How did it get out here?" "It was left in the safe cupboard over there in the central courtyard." "I don't see any cupboard!" "No, the cupboard has been destroyed. That pile of rubbish is what is left of it." No matter how Huntley pressured the professor it was clear that he had no answer that he could give. "Show me where the cupboard was." Huntley was led to the spot where the cupboard base was still bolted into the ground. "I must get on," said Murton. "You know your way out." The professor headed back the way that they had come and Huntley was relieved to see the back of Murton.

There was something about him that made Huntley feel uncomfortable. He looked around the yard, but the only other thing in that space was the backup generator. He spent some time looking at the massive box that at one time fitted into his pocket but there did not seem any explanation to the growth of it. He headed back to the office and wondered, on the way, about his reception at the lab and he concluded that it must be down to guilt or failure to discover anything about the box. Their lack of providing any answers must have been very embarrassing. Sir George was astounded by Huntley's report and he was not alone at being mystified by the changes to the box. The fact that such an originally small object could grow to such an extent was beyond comprehension. News had arrived about the activities of Judy Blain. She had headed for Wexford in southern Ireland and booked into the Ferrycarrig Hotel.

Huntley had been there many years before and had been impressed by the service and quality of his stay. The hotel overlooked a beautiful lake and the rooms and entertainment had been first class. The sense of isolation whilst at the hotel, sitting with a good quality glass of wine, looking out over the deserted lake, was excellent. While sitting and relaxing by the lake, there were no buildings, houses or roads to break the vista of the tree-lined lake. The fishing boats and pleasure boats gently rose and fell to the wind, creating a gentle swell of the water. He fondly remembered his visit and the feeling of total relaxation that he felt there. He looked forward to following Judy there in the near future but his hopes were dashed when Sir George insisted that he would leave it to the Irish group to sort.

Huntley did his best to argue his case for going, but he could not get him to change his decision. It did, however, give Huntley time to go back to the lab. And take another look at that box, if that is what it could be called now. His London flat overlooked the river Thames and was only a few hundred yards from the Palace of Westminster bridge. He always enjoyed sitting in the restaurant below his flat at Mario's, enjoying fine food and wine. He was sitting at his favourite table in Mario's as Mario approached him. "What is your speciality today, Mario?" "Good to see you, Huntley, we are doing 'Gnocchi al Forno' today." "Ah, baked potato dumplings with stringy mozzarella cheese, one of my favourites, but you look very down today, Mario. What troubles you?" "We have had a compulsory notice to quit the building, if you haven't had your letter about your flat, then you will get one soon. They are going to knock down this whole block and extend the Westminster building." "Never!" exclaimed Huntley, "that is pure vandalism. I wonder who dreamed up that plan?" "It seems that they are going to make this a new entrance to the Houses of Parliament for security reasons," explained Mario. "We have only two months to relocate, and there is little that we can do, but to celebrate our friendly and your patronage, I will join you for a glass or two of my finest Barbera D'Asti, a fruity, soft red wine. I will go and retrieve a bottle or two to drown our woes."

Mario came back to join Huntley as Mario's niece served them both their meals. "This is such a pleasure, Mario. I am really going to miss being here. We have been friends now for a long time but I hope that we will be able to keep in touch when the time comes to leave." "We will drown our sorrows in style, Mr. Huntley and look to a happy future." They savoured the wine when the lights suddenly went out. Mario struck a match and lit the table candles. "I will go and check what has happened to the lighting. After a few minutes, the lights came back on, and Mario returned. There was no explanation as to why the lighting had failed, but the electric system had been compromised, so Mario had turned off all but the electricity not used for cooking. They sat in the silence of the restaurant and peacefully enjoyed their repast. Later that evening, when Huntley returned to his flat, he had a flash of inspiration. Mario had said that the electric system had been compromised, and Huntley remembered the box growing when it was near his television. He wondered if there was a direct connection to the growth experienced when placed by the generator in the professor's yard. Maybe that was how the changes came about. The magnetic field created by the TV and the generator may be the reason for the changes.

Huntley hardly slept through the night and was up bright and early the next morning. He called the ministry store, booked out a hand generator, and almost ran to the laboratory. He insisted that he was alone with the box and made sure that no one could observe his activities. He switched on the generator and held it close to the silver shape, his heart pounding in expectation. Nothing happened, so he held the generator as close as possible, and the shape responded. He backed away, and the shape stopped changing. He tried the experiment again with the same result. The generator had a very low magnetic field, but even that had the desired effect. He had to get a more powerful magnetic field to be certain. He left without any explanation to the 'Boffins' only to return from the equipment store with a far more powerful generator and the security team that had been present previously. The team stood guard to ensure that no one from the laboratory could see what was going on. Huntley stood in front of the box, wondering how to proceed for the most positive results. He had concluded that the magnetic field created the changes but how to control those changes and possibly reverse them?

He approached the box with the strongest magnetic field that he could create. As he got closer, the box grew, but as he almost touched the box, a small hole appeared, and it continued to grow as he held the field generator close. For the first time, Huntley could see inside the box. He noticed as he stepped away from the box that while the hole grew, the box didn't. He could see inside the box through the hole what had caused the rattle. It was now very small in comparison to the box but it lay in the bottom of the shape. It was pyramid in shape and looked to be of the same material as the box but it had to have different characteristics somehow. Why was it inside of the box? Was it just to see if it could be put inside, or did it have some purpose? He stepped closer to the box to get a better view, but he forgot that the field was still active, and as he got level with the opening, it quickly closed. He had made contact with the surface of the box. The box, itself, reduced in size and made Huntley step back in surprise, and all movement ceased. Was the box playing games with him?

Reluctant to make any more mistakes, Huntley decided to risk touching the box again with the magnet on its surface, and the reduction was immediate. As long as he was in contact with the box with the magnet it continued to reduce in size. He switched off the magnet when the box was reduced to its' original size and put the box in his pocket. Taking the security team with him, he left the labs and instructed the team to return all the equipment to the store.

Huntley went to see Sir George, but he was out of the office, so Huntley poured a whisky and sank into one of the comfortable armchairs in the suite room. He felt that he needed to calm his nerves after his experiences with the box and felt it in his pocket just to make sure that he had not been dreaming it all. He was determined to keep the information away from the 'Boffins'. It seems that in the past, their type had caused all the aggravation and death involved with the box. He knew that it would cause problems when they discovered that the box had gone, but what Huntley had experienced was in the realm of science fiction.

Huntley became more relaxed after his third large whisky and Sir George returned as He filled his glass and a large glass for Sir George. "I suggest that you take a seat, sir and get a tight hold on your glass. You will be needing a drink when I finish telling you my discoveries." Huntley carefully and slowly told of the happenings and watched the jaw of his companion drop as he listened. When Huntley had finished his story, Sir George drained his glass in one swallow. They both sat in silence, thoughts racing through their minds. The implications were devastating and frightening, even though the full mystery of the box was still to be investigated. After a few more drinks and careful thought, Sir George broke the silence, "The Irish group has arrested Judy and her contact at the Ferrycarrig Hotel, and it looks as if we have the mastermind behind all of this in custody at last. It appears that the man in custody is Reuben King, the grandson of the cousin and assistant of Albert King, when Albert discovered the metal and created the box that came into your possession. Saville D. King was head of security here until a few years ago. He still had security clearance, and he also had access to all offices in our department, which means he had access to my stationery and signed documents that I had signed and cleared in the past. That explains how he could copy and impersonate my instructions to people in a variety of departments who had little to do with me on a daily basis. He had come across the experiments conducted on metals undertaken by Albert Reuben, and we now know why he was prepared to kill to get his hands on the box. In the commercial market, the knowledge of the box and how it could be used would be worth billions and billions of pounds. I have no alternative now but to talk to the prime minister about this case. I just can't keep it to ourselves anymore." Huntley was shocked, "I am not sure that it would be wise to involve anybody else with this information. We do not know enough about the box to let anyone else know of its existence. The properties will have military uses, and miniature weapons could be smuggled into a country without anyone being the wiser. Who can we trust with this? We just can't make it public yet. Give me more time to get to know the box better, and then we can discuss its future. One Saville D. King is enough without creating another one, and we might be the first on the list to be got rid of."

"Do you know, you are right in what you say,

Huntley. Duty, in this case, is not the priority. We will hold off for now and decide when we have more concrete evidence." "Thank you, sir. I really don't think that we can involve anyone, and I mean anyone, in this, particularly the 'Boffins' who are going to cause a great flap when they ask about the box. It would be funny if it wasn't so serious. I would love to see their faces when they look for a massive metal ball and find it gone." Sir George reassured Huntley, "I will deal with them when that happens."

Chapter 9

Huntley took the box from his pocket and a magnet from his other pocket, "Let's see what happens." He applied the magnet directly to the surface of the box, and the side opened completely. Huntley could see the small pyramid inside, and without thinking, he tipped it out into his hand. It was smooth and cool, and on inspection, he could see some markings on the side. "Have you a magnifying glass, sir?" He was handed a large glass from the desk and looked carefully at some writing on one side and some symbals on the other. On the base of the 'right' pyramid was a complex formula. "We will need a metallurgical chemist to decode this if we are to understand it, but who could we trust to do it?" "What are the symbals?" asked Sir George. "One is a set of concentric circles, and there is another set with a cross through it. The third one looks like a screw."

As they studied the symbals, the phone rang. It was the priority phone and Sir George answered immediately. He listened for some time before replacing the receiver. "That was a report from Ireland. Saville and Judy had been arrested on suspicion of murder, amongst other charges, and

Saville had requested his statuary phone call. When they came back to check on them, they were both dead. The medics confirmed death by potassium cyanide." "Well, we can't bring them to justice now, and hopefully that closes the case, but why request a phone call if you plan suicide?" asked Huntley. It was a question that they were both puzzled by, but it occurred to them both that there may be someone else who had been contacted and involved. It might not be over after all. They would have to wait and see what developed.

They returned to the box and the pyramid. Hours went by unnoticed, but they had more and more information on the properties of the box, and they were astounded by the strength and abilities that they discovered. Neither had noticed the time, and it was late in the evening, so they decided to call it a day. Huntley kept the box in his possession, and Sir George did not raise any objection, in fact, he thought it the best thing to do. If there was someone else involved his office may not be as secure as it might be. Before parting, they agreed that they would consider the case closed even though there was a possible doubt of some other person being involved, but the priority was to agree on what to do with the box. Back at his flat, Huntley kept the box with him at all times, and he didn't even trust it to his safe. Earlier, he had discovered how to control the box, open it, close it and stop any growth or change. He had also learned how to control the shape and had now made it flat-based and resembling a paperweight. He had taken a label from a bought item and stuck it on the base of the box.

Huntley slept well that night, rose refreshed in the morning, and quickly showered and dressed. He headed for breakfast in Mario's and realised that he had no plans for the day and, in fact, not for tomorrow either. He pondered on the fact that he had been so preoccupied with events that he had lost touch with all friends and relations, and he was now without any close family. Mario had his problems as he sat down with Huntley, who was conscious of the problems that Mario faced. They talked over their coffees and did their best to put the world right. Mario told Huntley that the restaurant was closing early today, and all of his family were coming together for a party to celebrate the happy years spent in the business. They were also going to plan the future by gathering ideas and considering possibilities. Huntley was invited. He was really happy to be invited and looked forward to meeting the family again, most of whom he knew. He thanked Mario and set off for a shopping spree in the city.

As he walked down Oxford Street, he came to a gent's outfitters and in their window was a pinstripe Italian suit. It looked the business so he went in and found that it was a perfect fit straight off the peg. He kept the suit on and carried his other clothes in the bag provided by the shop. He had never paid more than thirty pounds for a suit, but this one was worth every penny of the forty-five pounds that he paid for it. Huntley wandered around the city feeling more free and relaxed than he had felt for a long time. Was the case really closed? He dismissed the thought of the box and concentrated on strolling around without feeling any pressure. He walked and walked in the spring sunshine, passing through Leicester Square, Picadilly, Nelson's Column, Horse Guards Parade, and finally arriving in St. James Park, walking on to Westminster Abbey. It was late afternoon when he finally arrived back at his apartment. He showered and changed into casual clothing before heading downstairs to meet up with Mario.

It was strange to see the pavement outside of the cafe without a member of staff encouraging passersby to partake of the restaurant foods and drinks. The pavement tables had gone, and the windows were covered by curtains that had recently been put up as if to shut out the outside world. Other than the restaurant sign gave away that it was not a quiet nineteenth-century residential building. The embankment was quiet, but the traffic still crossed over Westminster Bridge. The lowering sun cast shadows, moving and shimmering on the Embankment and the river Thames. Few boats were moving on the river but a pleasure boat full of revellers was passing by. They were probably heading for Kew Gardens or even up to Hampton Court Palace. He turned and headed for the door of the restaurant, but as he approached, the door opened to reveal a smiling Mario, who gave him a warm welcome. "We are all here, and Gino was watching for you to arrive. Let me introduce you to all of our family. You know more of them, the boys, of course, you know, but I don't think that you have met my wife Bella and my daughter Gina. They are very rarely at the restaurant."

Huntley shook hands with Bella, but when he turned to meet Gina, he was stunned by her beauty, and his assured manner lost some of its control. An Italian girl, who was very pale skinned, and she had blond hair. She was in her early twenties, and when she saw the effect that she had on Huntley, she smiled an embarrassed smile. Mario and Bella exchanged a knowing look, and Mario dragged Huntley away to meet his brother and his wife, who did most of the restaurant meals. Huntley expressed his appreciation for their culinary skills, and Mario's brother soundly hugged him. Mario poured the drinks, and the music and chatter soon filled the room with happy sounds. In the melee, Gina and Huntley slowly gravitated together. Their eyes had met on a number of occasions throughout the evening and they gazed longer as the evening went on.

Finally, they met and spent the rest of the evening in each other's company until all awkwardness had gone, and they relaxed and enjoyed the rest of the night. They promised to meet the next day, and the next day became the next and the next. They were very happy together, and the fun became a romance, but a call cut their time together short one morning from Sir George, "Huntley, I need you in my office immediately. Whatever you are doing, drop it and get here as fast as you can! What I have for you is very important and urgent." Huntley contacted Gina and explained. They agreed to meet as soon as they were both free.

<u>Chapter 10</u>

The scene as Huntley arrived at the office took him by surprise, and the room was full of people. Senior Government officials, security officers and Sir George looked most uncomfortable. He was sitting at his desk, but on the wrong side; his usual seat was occupied by a most unpleasant-looking little man who addressed Huntley as he entered, "Ah, Haverstock, do come in and sit down." The only seat available was beside Sir George, who avoided eye contact with him as he took his seat. "Now, Haverstock, I believe that you have something that belongs to us. Your apartment is being searched as we speak, but my team has not found the box. You will tell me where it is." "I do not believe that we have met before, and as you have failed to introduce yourself, I think not." "Do not get smart with me!" exploded the little man as he leapt out of Sir George's chair. A large man stepped forward and said, "Maybe I can help to explain things here. I am the Right Honorable James Huneysuckle, M.P. Minister for Defence, Research and Development. The gentlemen here are the internal Westminster security team, and Mr. Smeaton is conducting and heading the investigation into the whereabouts of a certain object. Please continue, Mr Smeaton, and be more civil in your questioning."

Huntley watched Smeaton deflate at the admonition from the M.P., and he looked around at the stern faces of the security team, most of whom were trying to avoid a smile. He caught a glance from Sir George who gave a look of caution to Huntley. Huntley acknowledged the warning. "Well, Mr. Haverstock?" "What is it that you believe that I have that belongs to you?" "You came across a small metal box some time ago, and Sir George has confirmed that it is your possession." "Ah, that thing, yes, I am afraid that I do not know of its whereabouts. It was misplaced or dropped somewhere, and I have looked for it, but I have been unable to find it again. It was, as you say, just a small box of no real significance and very little value." There was a charged silence in the room, and Smeaton looked as if he was about to explode. Still, Huneysuckle stepped in again, "The box is of great value to us and was developed through government research and development jurisdiction in the north of England. It is something that we dealt with years ago, and a 'D' notice was applied to maintain secrecy. It was never to be let out of the top-secret unit ever. We do not know how you came to have it in your possession but I hope that you understand the gravity of the situation and give us your full co-operation."

Huntley considered his comments for a few moments, "I am quite concerned at the heavy-handed approach to getting any form of cooperation from us and the way in which you are treating us. Sir George and I are trusted and loyal servants of the Queen and Westminster, and the government owes a great deal to the services provided by Sir George and his team. Your methods seem to deem us some sort of criminals, but I have told you that the box has truly disappeared, and without any pressure from your team, I am sure that Sir George and I will give you all the support that we can." Huntley looked at Sir George, who nodded his approval. "We will do all that we can to return what belongs to you." Smeaton thumped the desk with his fist and drew himself up to his most diminutive height, but a raised hand from Huneysuckle pre-empted any outburst. "I believe that you are right, Mr Haverstock; how would you like to proceed with our discussion?" "Firstly, this security team is quite out of place and totally inappropriate, and Mr. Smeaton is not helping to provide a congenial atmosphere for discussion. I am sure that in a more

relaxed atmosphere, we can make progress."
Huntley took a breath and looked around the office.

Huneysuckle showed a fleeting sign of
frustration, but after a brief silence, he waved
Smeaton and his team out of the office. Huntley
tilted his head to Sir George to retake his desk chair.
As Sir George reclaimed his rightful position
Huneysuckle and his two aides sat down facing
him. "Thank you, Huntley. Would you gentlemen
care for a drink? Tea, coffee or something
stronger?" They all opted for something stronger.
As they drank their choice of drink there was a
feeling of relaxation not previously experienced.
Huneysuckle broke the silence, "Well, I believe that
you are both aware of the history of the box,
particularly you, Mr Haverstock, as your family
members were on the team that developed it. How
the box came to light again after it was classified
and secured, we do not know, but we know that
somehow it came into your hands, Huntley, but of
course, it is, after all, government property."
Huntley was aware from the use of his name that
Huneysuckle was trying to defuse the former
pressure. Huneysuckle continued, "It is highly
secret and must be handed over to the correct
section for safekeeping." Sir George replied,

"Huntley has told you that the box has disappeared and that he and I will do all that we can to retrieve it for you. Is that not correct, Huntley?" "It is, sir, but I must ask why such an insignificant object is of such importance?"

Huneysuckle's frustration showed itself again, but he took a deep breath, "The nature of the box is top secret and of national security, so I am afraid that I cannot divulge any information to you or anyone else. I will have to insist that you find it and return it to me without delay." Huntley knew, probably, more about the box than Huneysuckle did, but he said, "Very well, leave it with us, and we do our very best to trace it for you. That is all that we can do." The group opposite shuffled and whispered, but eventually, Huneysuckle and his aides stood and indicated that they were leaving, "As soon as possible, Sir George and I will hold you personally responsible." At that, they left the office. As the group left, they both sank into their chairs with great relief. "I need a refill." said Sir George, "and I am sure that you do too. You took one hell of a risk talking to them like that, and they will be watching your every move, mine as well. They will be watching for you to go to collect the box where ever you have hidden it." "What the hell is going on? You are the head of security. Who were those clowns?" "No clowns, Huntley. They are beyond security, and they are very dangerous. It is a group that neither of us want to upset. It is the first time that I have had proof that they actually do exist; before this they were just a story from legend. What have you done with the box?" "It is safe but I have no intentions of handing it over to them or anyone else until I get to know the score. You know some of the box's characteristics, but I have discovered a whole lot more. By the way, are we being monitored in here?" Huntley pointed to Sir George's desk. Sir George stared at his desk with a start, and he pointed at a desktop lighter that did not belong there. Sir George got up and waved Huntley to leave the room with him. He led the way to a secure interview room at the top of the building. "How did you know Huntley?" "I didn't recognise the lighter, and I know that you don't smoke. Are you sure that these people are on our side? How can we check on them?" "That will be difficult, Huntley. As I said, these people are phantoms, and not many even people know of their possible existance. I can tell you that Huneysuckle is genuine as an elected representative in charge of the Ministry for R and D. He has had to be checked again and again, but the rest of them, I don't know.

You said that you have found more out about the box?" "Yes, sir, but can I even tell you? Let me just say that with what I know, I could invade any country in the world, and they would know nothing about any invasion until it was too late to set up any defences." "What? You must be mistaken." Huntley shook his head, "No mistake, sir. It is no wonder that they want to get hold of it, and they obviously know some of its' capabilities. Anyone who has control of the box could hold the world to ransom. "Huntley, go and get the box, and we can't risk them finding it." "Okay, sir, but we can't keep calling it 'The Box'. Let's call it 'Mary'." "Excellent! First to get you out of here without being seen and followed."

<u>Chapter 11</u>

Sir George led the way back to the office and into one of the guest suites, one that Huntley had not seen before or even knew existed. In the bathroom was a full-length mirror. At the touch of a hidden switch the mirror rotated and allowed them to access the passage behind. Along the passage was a lift door. Sir George entered the code, and the lift door opened. At the same time, the mirror closed. They descended in the lift, and on opening, they were on the underground rail system. Sir George explained that Sir Winston Churchill had used this very system during the Second World War. It was now not used and many in government knew that it was there. Sir George led on along the rail track to another lift entrance. The lift ascended, and to Huntley's surprise, he was on the Embankment opposite Mario's restaurant. Huntley now knew how Sir George had frequently arrived to see him unobserved and unheralded. Huntley looked around and saw two men standing on the Embankment. We will have to come back later when it gets dark. The apartment is under surveillance, and there is no way of getting past them unobserved.

They retraced their steps and went back to the office to return as soon as darkness fell. Back on the Embankment, Sir George remained hidden in the lift entrance while Huntley crept unobserved in the dark to his doorway, which was set back in the shadow of the street lighting. He quickly went to his flat and found it an absolute mess. The place had been thoroughly searched and not a lot of care had been taken in the process. Draws had been emptied on the floor, cupboard contents strewn around, and the bed had been stripped, but amongst all the mess, the paperweight 'Mary' was on the floor. He couldn't risk carrying it out in case he was seen, and he thought for a while before he had a brain wave, moulded to his chest shape, and wore the thing like clothing.

Leaving the flat, he reached the downstairs door and saw the two men opposite on the Embankment. He looked to see Sir George still in the lift doorway. Huntley hadn't realised the lift was actually inside a police box. Huntley had seen police going in and out of the very same box on a number of occasions but had never really taken any notice of it. He waited for a while, and as the two men turned to watch some movement on the river, he headed for the police box. He had gone only a few yards when he heard a shout. He had been spotted so he ran as fast as possible and crashed into the police box and Sir George shut the door immediately. They descended in the lift. They both knew that they had been discovered, but Sir George just smiled. The men pursuing them forced their way into the locked police box only to find an empty police box. Nothing unusual at all, stone floor, standard equipment, but empty. Men appeared on the Embankment from all directions, searching for Huntley. They had no idea how he had evaded their trap.

Back in the office, they parted and went to their allocated quarters. Huntley couldn't sleep. He was expecting visitors at any time. They must be furious at being outsmarted, and he wondered what their next move would be. He reshaped 'Mary' and took the instruction key out to check for any more information. What else was written on it? He took the magnifying glass to look at the message on the base. It read: 'Never allow this to fall into the wrong hands, it is very dangerous!' Huntley wondered if it just meant what was written or did it have a specific meaning? On one side was written 'Texture by unlock magnetic contact'. What does that mean, thought Huntley? He decided to try and sleep on it, so he put the key back inside 'Mary'.

He looked around the room that Sir George had given him. This was not a room that he had known of previously. There were a number of guest suites, but this one was very grand. The building was very old and must have been a townhouse of some distinction years ago. The ceilings were very high and were decorated with plaster fruit and vines that looked as if they were hanging down, ready to be eaten. There was a family crest painted and highlighted with gold leaf or gold paint. The walls were all oak panelled, and the floor carpet was deep pile and very regal. There was everything needed for a pleasant stay: a four-poster bed, a bar, an en suite bathroom and a writing desk. Relaxing on the four-poster bed, Huntley slipped into a slumber and had some disjointed and disturbing dreams: the box, messages everywhere, the key, memories of his grandfather and the tales that he used to tell him when he was a child. Images of the old house that they had lived in with his grandfather during his early years and images of the forbidden understair cupboard. Being young and inquisitive, he had peeped into the cupboard on one occasion and seen what looked like a shiny bomb.

Huntley woke with a start with the realisation that that was 'Mary' under the stairs all those years ago. He was surprised that it was light and he had slept through all the night. He heard in the distance the sound of a telephone ringing and the voice of Sir George answering. He got up and quickly washed and dressed. When he joined Sir George, breakfast had been delivered, and Sir George was eating and reading the newpapers. Huntley looked at the full breakfast available on the table, a nice way to start the day. "Well, you are in demand this morning, Huneysuckle was demanding to know of your whereabouts yesterday evening. I assured him that you did not leave this building last night or at any other time since we talked to him. He seemed to be reluctant to accept my story, but I told him that we had been so concerned by the seriousness of the case that we had had a few too many drinks and that we had overslept to get over the indulgence." "That confirms that it was his men who were watching on the Embankment last night, but I have more to tell you about 'Mary'."

They finished eating in silence. "I had the office scoured for listening devices, and four were found and disposed of. They left the building by the main entrance and walked along Whitehall towards

Westminster Bridge. They knew that they were not alone, but they were well out of earshot, and Huntley went over all that he had recently discovered about 'Mary'. The main message on the key was: 'Keep this out of the wrong hands' and not allow anyone in power to get control of it. It gave too much power to those who could corrupt that power. He told Sir George that it could be changed into any shape or size and disguised as something quite harmless, but it could contain powerful and destructive contents. "It appears that my family members learned how dangerous it was and that this amazing material could be used to even destroy the world as we know it. They took great risks to protect the knowledge and keep it from anyone outside of their team, but somehow, their discoveries were leaked. I now realise why poor John was killed; he gave his life to protect the box, and he passed on the responsibility to defend it to me. He has made me the custodian of the box, and I have decided to keep the family tradition alive. I will be keeping the secret from everyone and I believe that you and I have the same responsibility to protect it.

I propose to let Huneysuckle know that one of his men found the box along with some other things that they took during their search. I will hide 'Mary' in a place that no one will ever find her." Sir George sat and looked at Huntley.

He said nothing and he was thinking hard about all that had happened. Eventually, he agreed with the plan, "Do not even tell me what you plan to do with her. I will back you with Huneysuckle, and we will head for your flat now and pretend to search. He will be aware that we have been there, and that will lend credence to our story. There were so many of his men involved that they would be running around like headless chickens for a lifetime, looking for the culprit. It also gets him off my back neatly. If we can get him to believe that one of his men has lost it somehow, then it may hopefully conclude this matter forever. Leave things as they are for a few days, and I will arrange another meeting with Huneysuckle. Let us both come up with a strategy for diverting attention away from us and onto his group."

<u>Chapter 12</u>

Huntley's thoughts turned to Gina. He would take a day or two away from London on the pretext of further enquiries. He could easily lose any would-be followers. When he got back to his flat, he went downstairs to visit the restaurant. Although the place was closed he was sure that he could get a meal with Gina's family. He was still wearing 'Mary' like a close-fitting vest, and he was surprised at how comfortable it had become. His knock on the door was answered by Gino, who gave Huntley a typical Italian-type hug in welcome. He was dragged upstairs to join the rest of the family. Gina was so pleased to see him again and hugged him as if it had been years since they had been apart. Huntley felt like a guest of honour as they sat down to eat. Gina told him that she was leaving for Italy the next morning to conclude some family business. Huntley quickly thought and said that he would be happy and honoured to escort her on her travels. He explained that he had a few days free and it would be great to see Italy and experience a little sunshine and warmth. The fact that he did not mention being with Gina did not pass unnoticed around the table, and knowing looks were exchanged. Mario was delighted to agree to them going together and that

Gina would not be alone. He went to get a bottle of his finest to celebrate and wish them well on their journey together.

They all toasted the couple, and Huntley got the distinct impression that Mario could hear wedding bells already ringing out. The thought had also occurred to him as the evening went on with happy chatter, dancing to loud music and drinking in steady supply.

Eventually, everybody retired to their beds, and the next morning, Huntley booked the same flight to Italy and they were in the air and on the way to Italy before lunchtime.

They landed at Fiumicino Rome airport in the early afternoon. They were met by Francesca, Gino's cousin and driven to the town of Fiumicino to the family restaurant Il More on the Via Delle Carpe. The restaurant overlooked a sizeable lagoon and, beyond that, the Tyrrhenian Sea.

Francesca and her family only spoke Italian, no English, so Huntley needed Gina to translate any conversations in which he was involved. The welcome was warm and friendly but that soon changed when Gina told the family how Huntley had joined her on this trip. The wine started to flow, and Huntley was treated like the prodigal son from there onwards, Gina was chaperoned constantly by Francesca's aunt. They spent the evening visiting the famous sights of Rome but spent much of the time at spots in the city not visited by by tourists. Gina pointed out the fiscal centre where she was to transact her business dealings on the following day. They went to the Castel Saint Angelo bridge and took a riverboat ride along the river Tiber. They sipped their drinks as they floated past the Palace of Justice and St. Peter's Basilica, all under the watchful eye of their chaperone. Gina explained that she was to pick up a family treasure the next day and fly back to London in the afternoon.

The treasure was necessary for the plans for all of the family. She was also to collect a present that was deposited for her when she was very young by her grandmother for the time when she reached a certain stage in her life. It was a small brush and comb in a shiny box. It was the next morning, and they were at the building where the bank representative opened the safety deposit box, and Gina collected all the contents. As they walked back, Gina showed him the box, and as she handed it to him, a man ran straight at Huntley. It was Huneysuckle. Shots rang out, and bullets struck

Huntley in the chest. He fell to the floor as if dead, assisted by the impact of the bullets. Huneysuckle grabbed the box and ran off. It all happened so quickly that Gina was stunned, and she froze as she saw Huntley lying on his back on the ground. She was sure that he was dead. As she started to recover, Huntley drew a deep breath and got to his feet. Gina looked at the holes in his shirt and her mouth dropped open in surprise as Huntley smiled at her. "You should be dead," said Gina. "You are right, but I took a few precautions just in case. Huntley smiled again, knowing that 'Mary' had saved his life. He was still wearing it like a vest. His hand went to his chest, and as he took it away, two flat bullets fell into his hand. He said nothing as he put the bullets into his pocket. Gina was full of questions and she was still shocked by the whole thing. Huntley explained that it was part of his job from time to time, and such risks can sometimes happen. He told her that he had been fully prepared for just such an attack. It occurred to him that if 'Mary' had alerted the airport security screening he may not have been wearing it. That was another characteristic of 'Mary'. The metal involved was surprising him all the time.

Huntley alerted the support team of events, and a search party was sent to find Huneysuckle. Gina was very quiet on their journey back to London and Huntley felt that she was more shocked at events than she had shown. She was very moody as they travelled back to the Embankment, and she did not invite him in. He went back to his flat but was very unhappy with the response from Gina and he hoped that it was not fatal for their relationship. He reported back to the office the next morning to be greeted by Sir George. "Good morning, Huntley. We thought that it was all over until that event in Rome but it appears not." "Any news on Huneysuckle, sir?" Unfortunately, no, the Italian police lost him at the airport. He was spotted by our team entering the airport, but from then on, it was the Italian police who took over." "He is going to be a bit upset when he finds the contents of the box that he took. It was a hair set, but he may believe that was how I disguised it. However, that will not last long. He is sure to discover his mistake." "I ran a further check on his background, and it seems that he is a metallurgical chemist and on checking his family, there was a member of his family who had dealings with Albert Reuben. During the war, his father was in the government's scientific research and development team. He has misled our security for years, and he has been trying to trace the box for as long as he can remember. I just wonder how many others there are who have some knowledge of its existence?" "Well, that confirms my decision. I am going to make sure that no one will ever get their hands on 'Mary'. No one can be trusted to use it for the good of mankind. It would appear that it just represents power and wealth. I am sorry but not even you will know what has happened to it." Sir George nodded his agreement. Huntley headed for the restaurant and was greeted by Gino, who handed him a note and told him that Gina had left the country that morning.

The family had also decided to relocate away from London, and preparations were well underway to leave. Gino shook Huntley by the hand with tears in his eyes. The door closed, and Huntley stood outside reading the note. Gina had been truly shocked by the events and felt that she could not spend her days with someone who faced such risks. She signed off with love but assured him that they would never meet again.

Huntley went into his apartment and headed for his bedroom, but as he approached, he noticed the bedroom door was ajar. The light from the bedroom window showed a shadow of someone standing behind the door. It was a scenario that he had planned for when he first took the booking. He had placed a small mirror high up in the bedroom that gave a perfect view of the rear of the door.

There stood Huneysuckle with a gun ready for action. Huntley went to his desk and took the power stun gun from the drawer. He approached the door and, without hesitation, fired at the door and the man standing behind it. The powerful stun lines passed through the thin panel on the door and struck its target. Huneysuckle fell to the floor unconscious. Huntley secured his hands and feet and called the office. A team arrived with Sir George within minutes of his call. Huntley searched his pockets and found the small shiny box, Gina's present. He would later drop it at the restaurant so that at least she would get her grandmother's sentimental present.

Sir George congratulated Huntley on his capture but that changed nothing. Huneysuckle would face the full power of the law, but there were others, so nothing was resolved. Huntley was invited to join him to report to the Prime Minister and a banquet later. The P.M. was assured that the box had been lost somewhere in all the happenings and that the information would be circulated to all departments who had any knowledge of it. Sir George received a commendation for his successful completion of the investigation and Huntley was also given recognition. They parted that evening, and Huntley told Sir George that he was taking leave and would be Freddy Goodchild again for some time. Sir George said that he was deserving of some time to himself but assured him that while he was head of security, his services would be required in the future.

The next day, Huntley headed north, not knowing what he would do, but he was determined to keep his promise to Lol and book them both a long holiday on the company finances. He started looking forward to planning where they were going, probably touring all the places that they had dreamt of as kids together at school. As he travelled up the M1 on his way home, a small cage containing a small pyramid swung gently on his car keys. He was confident that no one knew where 'Mary' had finished up, but in the Houses of Parliament, the lobby was full of M.P.'s and visiting public walking past the statue of Winston Churchill. He seemed to have been cleaned and polished to a shiny brightness. On close inspection, he also seemed to have a secret smile on his face.

www.ingramcontent.com/pod-product-compliance
Lightning Source LLC
Chambersburg PA
CBHW060805210726
48292CB00013B/1785